Finding Heraan

Tim Muirhead

Illustrations by Joy Benz

Copyright © 2016 words Tim Muirhead; illustrations Joy Benz

Published by Vivid Publishing
P.O. Box 948, Fremantle
Western Australia 6959
www.vividpublishing.com.au

National Library of Australia Cataloguing-in-Publication data:
Creator: Muirhead, Tim, author.
Title: Finding Heraan / Tim Muirhead.
ISBN: 9781925442311 (paperback)
Dewey Number: A823.4

All the gods, all the heavens, all the world, are within us. That is what myth is.

— Joseph Campbell

Translator's Introduction

The original manuscript of what you are about to read turned up on a wild winter's beach in Australia's South West. It was in a casket, like a treasure chest, half buried in the sand. I found it.

You don't believe me. You think I made it up. Ah now; perhaps you haven't been to the wild winter's beaches of the South West. Magic happens there. You can step, unknowingly, right into your soul so that the waves and wind and endless skies become a part of you and wash you clean. Giant whales leap lightly from the ocean, dolphins dance in symmetry on towering waves. Birds hover, exactly stationary, on buffeting winds. Receding waves leave glistening lines of silver on white sand. Great sculptures of water explode from the rocks and hang in the air, just for your joy. You can hold a handful of sand that, since the very beginning of the universe, no other hand has touched. And you won't even know.

Go there sometime. Step into your soul. You'll find magic. You may even, like me, find your own treasure. But if you don't, enjoy the waves. They are enough. The waves are enough.

My treasure, this manuscript, came in a language that has taken me over a decade to decipher. The language is not known to any linguists. It seems to have its roots primarily in the Indo-European languages, yet with elements relating to Indigenous languages of all continents. Where "the Kingdom" is cannot be determined. I can't even verify that it really existed at all, or that this entire manuscript isn't all an enormous hoax. But the words, as they emerged from the mists of an unknown language, gave me hope and strength in a troubled world. So, hoax or no hoax, I give you, here, my translation of the words written who-knows-when, in a Kingdom who-knows-where, by people who are little more than names on paper. Names on paper and yet, for me, flesh and blood, in a time and place; as though they live within me.

My work of translation has not been easy. It has taken me deeper into the labyrinths of freedom; deeper into the rich confusion of being human amongst others. For a time I became strangely haunted — stifled even — by the Faereen's curses and the indifference of many. There were years where the collection of strange writings, including Wistoria's story, sat in the dusty darkness of their chest, left carelessly in the cellar beneath my house.

But slowly, over the years, the Gnomic woman's words called to me. Slowly, the Stableboy's journey became my own. And in the end I knew that, having found this strange tale, I owed it to the Heranians, to Gabriel, to Sophia and Lodima, indeed to all the people of the Kingdom, to put it before others. And of course, I owed it to Wistoria. I cannot know but I have come to believe that, for Wistoria, revealing this story was her life's work.

So here it is: a gift to you from an awkward, fumbling translator in the hope that it will, in its small way, draw you to reflection, as it did me.

Tim Muirhead
Perth, Western Australia 2016

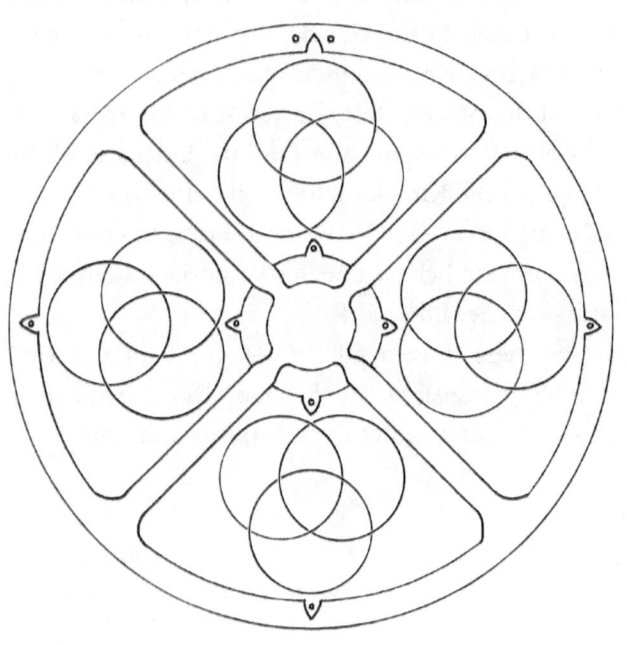

THE STABLEBOY'S JOURNEY

A Tale of Truth

By Wistoria of the Court

PREFACE

There are some — students of philosophy and the people of Heraan — who know and love, even today 'The Rings of Heraan' or 'Casandra's Rings'. But few know the story of how they, and the message they hold, were found, carried and delivered.

When I was young I met an aged man: Ageres. I had heard him spoken of as a man of insight, as well as an excellent Stable Master. But this was my first meeting with him. He was attending to my horse, who had become ill, and we were conversing. He said, in passing, "Speaking truth is not as simple as it sounds!" I felt a story behind the words and asked to hear it. He gave me the barest outline of his journey. His story resonated within me, as though I had been to similar places, and through similar trials. So I sought, and was granted, the Queen's permission to search deeper and further, finding others who held memories of Ageres, and piecing together the story you are about to read. It has taken me a lifetime.

Of course it is told through the mists of time, the illusions of memory, and the distortions of an old woman's hopes and dreams and grievances. Of course, as you read, you see a world within me, as much as you see places and people and events as they truly were. I confess: words that, in life, would surely have tripped and danced and stumbled, have been reduced here, to monologues — crafted merely to express their meaning.

So facts and figures and words may have been distorted in the telling. But I have tried, with all my heart, to reveal the truth within the tale.

Wistoria of the Court.

1

Sophia's Gift

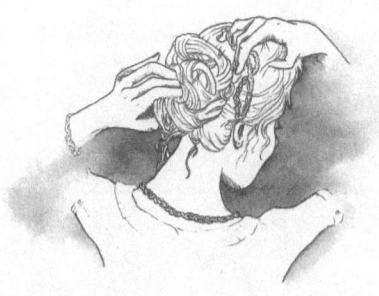

Ours was a Kingdom where magic and wonder were still known, but only to those who chose to see.

It lay beside a deep ocean, whose horizons flickered and sparked with the wings of dragons that flew between places unknown. Only the bravest seafarers had ever seen into the eyes of the dragons, and it was said to be the most wonderful and the most terrible experience of their lives. But this, as it turns out, is not a story of seafarers. Or of dragons.

The land that rose from the ocean's wild, glistening shores was bright with colour and bustling with life. It held jungles dripping with growth and shadows, and patchwork fields swaying with the love of custodians' hands. It held forests and woods full of wonders to be found, and fairies and elves just out of eyeshot. It held red and glaring deserts, all silence and emptiness and hidden scamperings. And high mountains, whose crowns were barren and whose feet were life itself.

The colours of the flowers, the flight of the birds, the chaos of the butterflies, the endless cycle of life and death: these were part of the magic, but they were not the magic.

The glowing of the moon and the power of the oceans, the searing sun and the soothing rain, the breezes and winds, the rivers and streams, the endless, endless, flow of life through the veins of tree and creature alike: these were part of the magic, but they were not the magic.

The magic could not reside alone in any corner, or jungle, sea or field. It sprang from every creature and every plant, every rock and pool of water. But only in the spaces and connections between them could the magic take hold. And alas, the magic was in danger. For division had begun to deplete the land. Yet only few could see.

The lands of our Kingdom rose, in their different ways, to a great 'Ring of Mountains' capped as white as the clouds, with hillsides of greens and faraway blues. This Ring of Mountains almost encircled a high, broad, lush valley.

Long ago, the valley had held a thousand brooks and a dozen streams that had danced their way toward one great, swirling waterfall which dropped away towards the lands below. But, generations ago, the people of the valley had built a dam above the waterfall, and created a large, still lake. On the shores of this lake now stood a busy, rushing, smoking City, all straight lines and ingenuity and noise.

This City was a wondrous place. It was the culmination of all that the people of the high valley — generation on generation — had strived for. The miracle of invention was alive and flourishing. The forces of nature were humbled by technologies that outshone the most powerful magic. The people were comfortable beyond the imaginings of their forebears. Humanity, it seemed, was in charge. Yet a few could see: all was not well.

This was in the time of King Gabriel.

Our Kingdom had long been guided by wise and compassionate monarchs, and our lands and people had flourished in their love.

There was mystery and awe around the kings and queens. Some said that they were, in fact, the many faces of one, immortal Lord. Others, that the one blood of truth and greatness simply flowed through their separate and newly born veins, one to the next. But all agreed: their reign was immortal; the knowledge of past and future was in their bones. And, when they listened well, they could hear the voice of all that was within them, and around them, and beyond.

Now King Gabriel, in his wisdom, was greatly troubled. He could sense that the people of his land were somehow faded, and the magic of his land somehow frayed. There was busy-ness and noise and activity, but his people seemed lost, distracted, diminished. Some seemed to know and feel this within themselves. Others did not, but simply blamed others so that conflict and bitterness grew.

And so the King was troubled. His reflections and his meditations, his readings and his calculations, his logic and his deepest thought could not ease his trouble, nor cast light on the decay that puzzled him.

Finally, then, he gathered his wisest advisers — seven in number — and put his troubled question. "Friends, I fear my Kingdom is in disarray. I feel its pain yet cannot name it, and so cannot heal it. What shall I do to make my Kingdom whole once more?"

His advisers responded, one at a time, without question or interruption, as was their way.

The first adviser, a man of economics, said these words: "Lord, your people have fear in their hearts. They fear that they may not know comfort in the future or that their children may live in poverty. They fear that others' wealth may exceed their own.

"But do not trouble yourself Lord. We will manage the Kingdom's finances so that all will prosper. Some may know troubled years, but soon wealth will create itself and recreate itself, and your people will be happy once more."

"I am pleased," said the king, but his heart remained silent, and troubled.

The second adviser, a man of technology, said these words: "Lord your people are bored, and dissatisfied. As the wealth of your Kingdom flourishes their demands for entertainment and comforts grow ever greater.

"But do not trouble yourself, Lord. Our ingenuity and technologies know no bounds. We are inventing machines for their entertainment, and mechanisms for their comfort. Nature recedes before us — the weather need not burden our bodies, nor silence nor stillness burden our soul."

"I am pleased," said the king, but his heart was still silent, and troubled.

Other advisers followed: a man of psychology, another of education, and then of politics, and then of science. Each spoke of answers. Each spoke confidently of what would come to pass if their advice were heeded. And to each Gabriel replied, truthfully, "I am pleased". But his heart remained silent, and troubled.

Then the King turned to the seventh of his advisers whose name was Sophia. She was a young woman. She shone with wisdom and her hair flowed like water. She had been chosen by the King — against the advice of other men — to speak of the future.

Sophia spoke quietly; gently. Yet her words, rising from someone so young and true, have echoed and grown down the years like a sermon that people are always longing to hear.

"Lord, your advisers are knowledgeable men. Their plans for change have truth within them, and will bring rewards. Of course you should heed their words and take from them what is true. Yet, alone, these plans cannot succeed. They speak of healing the branches of the tree, as the trunk decays from within.

"When we see the tree dying, shall we try to revive the leaves in one room, and the flowers in another; the branches and the roots and the bark all in separate rooms, and by separate means? What hope should we have of true healing if we separate the parts of the tree in this way? And even if there were hope, what point the healing, if the tree is thus scattered?

"For the tree is one. The illness of each part is the illness of the whole, and the illness of the whole becomes the illness of each part."

The King, with despair and hope, saw that this was so. He said to Sophia: "Your words resonate; I feel their truth. But what is the source of this illness that eats at the whole and the parts?"

She replied, "The *Spirit* of the people, and the *Spirit* of the land, is choking.

"It is like breath, this Spirit — the breath of life — for any of us and all of us. When our Spirit is choked we become like a person drowning and choked of air…

"The drowning person thinks of nothing but the next moment; thus do your people lose sight of the past, the present and the future. Thus do they lose sight of the deeper vision and wonder of living. Thus are they distracted by trivia.

"The drowning person lashes out at those who come near and, even as he seeks help, strikes at those who would rescue him. Thus do your people strike at each other and lose sight of others' needs, and see fear and enemies where love and friends should dwell.

"The drowning person grasps at anything to help fill the choked and airless space inside. Thus do your people consume too greedily of nature's gifts, and seek desperately for greater wealth and more distractions.

"Finally, Lord, the drowning person gives in, ceases to care, surrenders to this loss of breath, of

Spirit. Thus do your people finally choose apathy; carelessness. Passion, and compassion, die."

Sophia paused, as if waiting for a response from the King. But he offered mere silence. Silence, and his full attention. The other Advisers were also silent, but seemed uncomfortable, as though Sophia was answering a question that no-one had asked.

In the silence, then, Sophia went on.

"Lord, your Kingdom is awash with people drowning for lack of Spirit; unable to breathe life. Many still struggle. Some are able to call out. Most are agonising in silence — alone and resigned as a person drowning.

"And the ailment spreads itself, Lord. Thinking only of the next moment, we choke the future and the world around us. Lashing out, we spread fear and pain. Grasping, we feed our greed, while the simple needs of others and of nature — now and to come — are starved. Surrendering, giving in, ceasing to care, we turn away from the glorious potential of human life together. And so the Kingdom and the future slowly sink beneath the 'next moment' of each person. The whole Kingdom, then, is choked of Spirit."

At last, the King responded. "Yes, I see this. Choked Spirit chokes Spirit. The ailment of each person ails the Kingdom, and the ailment of the Kingdom ails each person." He could feel the truth in Sophia's words, and it troubled him even more deeply. "But how has it come to this?"

Sophia paused and closed her eyes, listening within. Then she spoke, slowly, as if repeating what she heard there.

"What is now is what we have chosen. We cannot choose a different now, only a different future.

"You have given your people great freedom. But freedom is hard. We ignore its call, ignore its challenge, and so do not discover how we might thrive on its gifts. We, the people, must discover, sometimes painfully, how to make such freedom work for us; how to breathe Spirit into our lives; how to seek wholeness and nourishment rather than disconnection and distraction.

"Too many, Lord, have seen freedom merely as a release from constraint, an invitation to aimlessness. They are adrift on an ocean: released from their mooring, but to what end? Released from our mooring we can choose, or we can drift. If we choose and set directions, choose and set sails, we can journey to rich and wonderful places. But if we do not choose, and choose well, the ocean may not be kind. At best, we will drift. At worst: well, we may long for the mooring."

"And so, dear adviser," the King asked with growing anticipation, "tell me: how do we repair this choked Spirit? What programs shall I implement?"

Sophia's eyes opened, as though startled.

"Gabriel — that is not the question!"

Her tone shocked the other advisers, and the King himself tightened. There was silence; hard, brittle silence. Only breathing could be heard beneath it. Finally, out of the silence, Sophia's voice emerged.

"The questions are many, and deep. But they are not of repair and programs, and will not be answered in this Court. They lie deeper, Lord. Deep in the soul that yearns to nourish us all.

"Your advisers' proposals hold truth. But if, as we act on them, we ignore the Spirit of people, the action will not bear fruit. Worse, it may do damage. It may rub at the fraying and fading that ails your people and your Kingdom."

The King, though restrained, spoke sternly: "I am used to receiving advice from Advisers. Yet you turn away from answers and action, and offer only mystery!"

Sophia appeared to falter. Momentarily, she shrunk back. But then she straightened, as though lifted by others behind her. "Mystery, but also truth. I have spoken of what I know. Beyond that, I will not offer you answers. Perhaps they lie within you, for the blood of immortality runs through you. Or perhaps they lie deeper still. But I will not offer answers beyond this that I know: that without Spirit, all else will fade and fray."

Tension still filled the Court. Sophia stood silent, then closed her eyes as if, again, asking questions of a voice within. When she opened them again, they were as clear as the wind.

"I can offer one small gift, King Gabriel. Three ribbons, handed down to me in silence by mothers' mothers. We have always known that the time would come when they could safely be handed to a true monarch. The time is here."

With this she reached for three ribbons of braided threads — ancient, tattered and worn. One of the ribbons sat upon her head, holding her flowing hair. One lay around her neck, arcing down as though embracing her heart. And the third graced her wrist, held there by her strong, sure hand. "Take these threads," the young Adviser said, "wear them, lord, and seek truth where you will."

The ribbons were simple and worn, but the King received them with grace.

He thanked all of his advisers — politely but with a heavy heart — and bade them leave him. He was tired and confused, and he retired to bed in the hope of rest.

Rest would not come. Sophia's words echoed in his heart. And with them, a slow, simmering anger began to rise. 'Who is she to name the ailment, and yet have no cure?' he thought bitterly. 'What sort of adviser is she that burdens her king with questions, but offers no solutions?'

He rose from his bed and paced the room, speaking aloud into the darkness. "The six, at least, offered answers to the problems they saw. And yet this young woman, so soft of hair and gentle of eye, shattered the comfort of their words, and left the debris with me, littering my sleep and my peace."

"Tomorrow, she will be my adviser no longer. I already have the advice of 6 learned men. I was foolish to think that she had anything to offer." Finally, with that dark thought, he slept.

And he dreamed of truths; truths that he had always known, yet never seen, nor spoken.

In his dream, the three ribbons of Sophia were brought to him on a velvet cushion — lying soft and circular, like rings. They were laid in such a way that the three became seven, and all the colours of the rainbow were in them.

On seeing them, his simmering anger exploded and, in his dreaming, he was unconstrained. He took the ribbons and threw them to the winds of the cyclone, but they blew back and dropped at his feet. He cast them into the fire of the volcano, but they flew out again, and fell at his feet. He hurled them to the depths of the oceans, yet the waves lightly carried them and, once again, they fell at his feet. He buried them deep in the earth and turned away, yet when he returned to his throne, the ribbons were there, and lay, still, at his feet; gentle rings of thread.

And the three formed seven, and all the colours of the rainbow were in them.

The King, in his dreaming, was now wild and thoughtless with rage. He grasped the circles of ribbon, and threw them in anger at the faded cross that hung above his throne; the cross that, for generations, had marked the four directions of the Kingdom, flanked by the ancient star and the crescent moon. To his amazement, rather than falling to the ground, the three became twelve, and the seven became twenty-eight. And rather than colours, words appeared; simple, familiar words. Strong words. Shining words. Words of Spirit.

He awoke with a start, just as the first light was appearing on the new day. And his heart, at last, was alive with hope. Gabriel, the King, had a message for his Kingdom.

As soon as the sun was over the horizon the King called Sophia to his court. "Sophia you are surely wise, and your ribbons are gold. They have brought me a message of truth and hope; a message of such simplicity that the humblest servant can grasp its meaning and the most arrogant politician cannot deny it. Will you stand with me on the balcony when I deliver the message to my people?"

Sophia was pleased for the King and spoke in her strong, gentle way again: "Lord, I can see, by the glow of your heart, that you have heard truth. I can see it is clear and pure, as though God has spoken within you. All who can hear it will be enriched. But it is truth. It cannot be delivered from high balconies."

Gabriel's pleasure turned immediately to frustration. "I am the King! If I don't speak, who will?"

To which Sophia responded: "You are the King. If you speak, who will question?"

The King paused, turning Sophia's response to understand it; struggling to see it from new angles. But then he went on. "Sophia, for me to know, and not to speak — this would be dishonest."

She replied: "Not dishonest. Patient. The tree grows from a patient seed. The seed falls from the patient tree. And forests rise. Truth is a seed from which forests might grow, not a mere image of a tree that people might bow down to. Spirit led from the throne or the pulpit will quickly choke or fester.

"Words from above will speak to people's fear. They may take them as rules; certainties that they are bound to follow, or bound to reject. Better that they can hear with their hearts, and know they are free to accept the words or ignore the words, as they choose. Then, truly, the words become powerful; gifts of the Spirit, rather than proclamations of the Court; whisperings of the heart, rather than mere instructions of the intellect.

"Lord, the power of the Court that is vested in you holds danger if used without care. People may listen to you with their fear, or with their need. It is better they listen with their own wisdom, where truth can be heard. Truth will develop Spirit. Proclamations may choke it."

"But still — it is my place to lead!" said Gabriel.

"If you wish to lead, give space for people to hear truth. Do not clutter them with certainties. Give space for truth, and let the message go where it will."

The King remained confused. "I have truth within me. Shall I speak, or not?"

"Speak, Lord, but speak with a voice that can be heard and questioned. Truth emerges best like sunrise; its first light shines from the edges. From the edges of experience. From the edges of consciousness. From the edges of conformity. From the Edges of your Kingdom. Let the message spread, dear Lord, and let it spread from the Edges, so that it may be truly heard; so that it may bring renewal."

And the King saw, at last, direction in Sophia's words. "But how shall I get the message to the Edges? What great person can I trust to be the courier of this sacred truth?"

Sophia responded, first, with silence. Long silence. And the King, becoming accustomed to her ways, waited with patience. Finally she responded, speaking slowly, as though choosing each word with care: "You will need a messenger who can travel well, and can be trusted to go to the farthest and strangest corners of the Edges. You will need a messenger who people will listen to without fear or awe. You will need a messenger who will not seek to interpret the message through his search for power. You will need a messenger who has humility enough to know that his is not the only way and so will respect, rather than fear, the truths of others.

She paused, silent again. Then her eyes opened with a smile, and she held Gabriel with a bright, strong, easy gaze: "May I suggest the humble Stableboy?"

11

The Messenger

Within the hour the Stableboy stood before the King.

He was, in truth, both boy and man; still in that time of mystery and confusion that turns the child to adult.

He had, since he could carry a brush, been stable-boy to his Grandfather, the Head Groom. They were charged with keeping the Court's stables, and tending to the horses within. The lad's love of the horses was deep from the first, and his knowledge and skills grew beyond his age. When the old man passed, the boy, though just sixteen, was naturally promoted, and entrusted with charge of the stables.

But titles, like habits, take time to change. And so to most in the City — even to himself — the lad was still, and perhaps would always be, 'Stableboy'.

Now he stood before the King, who beheld a humble lad — simple and honest, with a quiet nervousness that he made no effort to hide. The odour of sweat and straw and earth was upon him. His clothes were of the autumn, his hair a tangled shrub, his eyes a pond, undisturbed.

Gabriel looked on him with a powerful, gentle

gaze, and smiled. "What is your name, lad?"

"'Ageres, sir."

"'Ageres'!" the King repeated with delight. "A good name! It speaks of agency. It speaks of action and movement, and you have much to do and far to go. Be my agent, young Ageres! I have a message of truth for my people. Yet I do not have the power to have it heard. So, Ageres, you must carry it to the Edges for me. You must find the places where people are alive and open and do not insist on the main path. You must take it to people who will hear, and speak. And you must give them my message, and let the words spread as they will."

"But Lord, I have never travelled alone beyond the Ring of Mountains. How shall I ride far and fast enough to reach the Edges?"

The King said, "You need only reach for the fire within you, and it will drive you forward."

"But Lord, I am a mere Stableboy, with no title, and no bearing. Why will people listen to me?"

The King replied, "Speak the truth, and it will be heard by those in whom it dwells."

Ageres remained uncertain. He opened his mouth as if to express a third doubt, but then held his silence. So the King gave him the message. He drew the three Rings so that the three became seven, and they shone with each colour of the rainbow.

He showed the boy how to spread them around the cross of the compass, with the Call at the centre, so that the three became twelve, and the seven became twenty-eight. He told him the words that made beauty truth, and watched as Ageres's eyes shone with recognition.

The young man felt held and moved beyond his understanding, like the strings of the lute that cannot help but resonate to the sound of the bell, or the flower that cannot help but open to the sun's rays. The King's message seemed to awaken the sleeping dreams of his hope. It gave shape and voice to truths that he had felt, but could not name. He was awash with feeling.

But to the King he simply said "Thank you Lord. Your message is true."

"Then take it to the Edges, Ageres, so that others may hear. To help you in your travels and your speaking, let me pass on these three ribbons, from which the Rings of the message were born. Hold them safe. May they help you remember this place and this moment; this source of the message you now carry."

He handed Sophia's tattered, beautiful, woven threads to Ageres.

The boy looked at the mysterious gift he had been given, and back to the King's smiling face. "I will try to carry your ribbons, and your Rings, well."

With that, the King embraced the Stableboy as a

brother, and then laughed as, eyes still sparkling with recognition, the lad stumbled out of the Court, staring at the ribbons, and tripping over his own boots.

'Sophia was right,' thought the King. 'My message is in good hands.' And so he turned, once again, to his daily duties.

Ageres was bursting and bubbling to begin his quest. But his stables, and the horses within, called him first. So he did, first, what must be done; did it with the ease and ability of one whose very heart knows each task.

He set about brushing down all the horses and bidding them farewell. He fed each beast with their favourite grain and swept their stable clean. He took those horses that needed new shoes to the Smith, who gave them the love of his skills with iron. He repaired the loose shingles in the roof, and the gaps in the crooked boards. He filled the trough with fresh water, and laid the floors with fresh hay. And finally he trimmed the dead branches from the trees that shaded the horses in summer, let the sun warm them in the winter, and gave beauty to their eye.

As Ageres did all this he kept his dearest friend and most trusted assistant, Gregory, at his side. He spoke to him in an easy flow of quiet, clear words, explaining every task: how it was done, and what it meant to his beloved horses. As he spoke he could see in Gregory's eyes the light of love that he himself felt for these majestic beasts. By nightfall Ageres knew that his assistant would keep them well in his absence.

With that knowledge, the Stableboy slept sound, ready for his quest.

In the morning, before first light, he prepared his chosen horse — a mare called Sihdra. He loved her most amongst the horses; felt complete, easier, more open in her presence. She was pure and free; gentle and powerful; loyal and independent. She had no need to control, nor to submit. It occurred to Ageres as he brushed her coat: Sihdra seemed to embody that element that was the very essence of the King's Message — 'Spirit'.

He knew, then, that he could use the simplest, lightest rope bridle to guide her. She would heed his call if the call was clear and pure, so the simplest bridle would be enough. And he knew, from his Grandfather's teachings, that to journey long, he must journey light.

The Main Path to the Edges has always led from the western boundary of the City. It drops quickly out of the Ring of Mountains, then follows the long winding curves of the Great River in a quiet, patient loop that is easy to follow, and keeps away from harsh and hostile places.

But by this path it takes many weeks to reach the Edges in the east. And Ageres, enthused by the beautiful new Message of truth that he had received, was impatient.

He had long heard talk of a faster way to the Edges and the Ocean. Many travellers who came to the stables told stories and drew maps in the sand. "Why take the long slow journey around the Kingdom," they would ask with a laugh in their voice, "when the Edges and Ocean lie directly across the mountains and plateaus to the east?" Only later would Ageres realise that these travellers had all arrived from their journey in early spring. Only later would he realise that different seasons call for different actions and offer different gifts, and that summer was upon him.

So, in his enthusiasm for his quest, he set out for the eastern edge of the Valley, where the Dawn Pass lay beckoning, nesting comfortably between the two great peaks that shaded the City each morning.

Only one person noticed him leaving. She stood at her window where, every morning, she greeted the dawn. Her skin and her soul and her eyes were warmed by the new sunshine and hope of early morning. "Ride well, Ageres. Ride well. You carry the future with you."

But of course Ageres did not hear Sophia's words, nor feel her gaze. He was alive with the Message. Alive, too, with the strength of the beast beneath him and the lure of the jagged horizon ahead and the sun's first light, calling him forward.

They made their way quickly through the City streets and into the countryside. Soon they joined the Eastern Way — the steep, well-marked path that City Dwellers have always used to climb out of the valley and into the rich highlands beyond. But, though many others had travelled it before, it all felt magical and new to Ageres.

His senses — on this morning, and on this journey — were fresh and open and sharp and clear. He saw each bright flower, each green and budding leaf; heard the song of birds and the shuffling of creatures; smelt the decay and growth of the forests on the hillsides — all as though for the first time. Every element of life seemed an un-imagined miracle. He was awash with nature's fullness.

Every tiny detail sang of the beauty of the whole world. And the whole world seemed to welcome him in. Like a stream welcomes a raindrop, or a forest welcomes a seed.

By mid-afternoon, after a long, weaving climb, they reached the Dawn Pass. Standing together, clouds for breath, they looked silently back into the Valley. The boy's memory and his comfort rested gently in that valley and he grieved silently. Yet his very grieving gave him pleasure. For it hummed to the rhythm of his heart that, already, was bounding on toward the Edges.

As Ageres reflected, Sihdra simply stood and waited — her being, her moment, her past and her future complete.

Soon they turned to walk on. Before them, to the east, they could see the lands known as 'The Higher Fells'; an enchanting mosaic of woods and fields, farms and fences, cottages and villages that rest beyond the eastern flanks of the Ring of Mountains. The path at their feet, though, was steep and rocky, and the air was growing cold. So they began to carefully pick their way down from the Pass, towards the gentler lands below and beyond.

III

The Curse

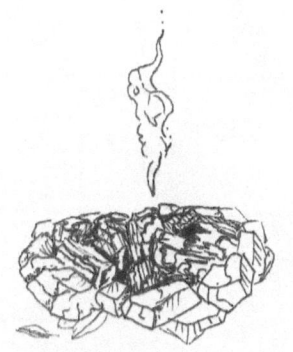

The Crusade

They made good progress and camped that night by a dancing brook that ran through a small wood. The fruits and seeds of the wood fed them well, the ground was soft and the air was soothing. Ageres made a small fire and stared into its flames, holding the ribbons that the King had given him and pondering the powerful Message that he had received. Soon, though, he fell to sleeping. The moon was full and his sleep was fitful, but he sensed nothing of the strange happenings that befell him that night...

Just as the last ember turned grey and cold, a strange, troubled wind drifted into the small clearing where Ageres slept. But it was no wind. Ageres was visited by a ghostly Faereen.

Many beyond our Kingdom will not hear of Faereens, dismissing them as superstition and imaginings. We in the Kingdom pay no mind: we know of their being and their damage. We know and despise their festering fragments of mean, mouldering magic. We witness their presence as they penetrate and expand the cracks of fear and doubt within us and around us, and there feed.

They are not beings of flesh, but of gases and vapour. Some have seen them; most merely felt them. But they are most dangerous when they are neither seen nor felt. It is said that they dwell most numerously in the tangled undergrowth of the slopes that lie just beyond the Ring of Mountains. Though perhaps it is simply that this is where they are most often seen or felt. Who knows?

What is known is that, being of gas and vapour, they can enter human being when the being is vulnerable. Like the tiny ants might feed off the body, but need it first weak or dead, so the Faereens feed off the Spirit, but need it first weak, or choked. And so, when they sense the opportunity — when someone is lost, isolated, diminished — the Faereens are at the ready, giving all manner of promises and dreams, delusions and distractions to fill the space where the Spirit should be. Then, having filled the space, they can draw at will on the energy of their victims; feed from their distraction, their bitterness, their powerlessness, their apathy.

Now many in the Kingdom have thought the Faereens' powers strong and startling. But they are not. Where human Spirit breathes free, the Faereens cannot enter. Where courage and humility dwell, they cannot feed. Yet nor can they rest. For if Spirit were to grow and spread, one being to another, Faereens would wither and fade. Instead, they must resort to their only remaining power: they must silence the voice of truth.

And so, on this night of the full moon, a Faereen skulked invisibly into the clearing where Ageres lay sleeping, and listened for his breathing, and his dreams.

It saw, immediately, that it could not enter, for this Stableboy was strong in Spirit. But it also saw the powerful message that rested within. It saw the rings, the cross, the colours and the words; the three and the seven, the twelve and the twenty-eight. It saw all this, and it felt even more. It felt truth and clarity. Truth and clarity that touched the heart; truth and clarity that shone like a light that all had seen yet never named; truth and clarity that burned like a flame, pure and bright enough to rekindle the Spirit of all who heard.

'And so', thought the Faereen, 'it must be silenced.'

Grunting and snarling like the creaking of old trees, pacing and worrying like a wind that keeps changing, the Faereen cast about for a spell that could defeat such a message. What trickery could weaken this truth that sat, pure and shining, within this lad's strong heart? What doubts and fears could penetrate the simplicity of such truth? Searching, despairing, it stared deep into the Stableboy's being, looking for the weakness in his Spirit, but finding none.

"But it must be stopped and it must be stopped, and the Spirit must never hear," the Faereen chanted to itself, over and over. It stared at the face of the boy and felt for the tension and trouble that ran up and down his spine, and in and around his heart.

Suddenly the answer came — came in the sight of an anxious frown and a tense tightening of the arms and legs. Suddenly the Faereen saw, in the boy, not doubt in his message but doubt in his self — in his own authority to carry such a message. *There* was the tangle of fear that it could scratch at, and work its magic. All it had to do was erase this boy's memory — not of the truth itself, but of the very source of the truth. For if the Stableboy thought that the message came from himself alone, rather than from a higher, older authority, then, surely, he could not carry on.

The Faereen skulked forward and swept the threaded ribbons from the boy's hand like a wind. And then cast its curse:

"You who shovel shit and straw and sleep with bridled beasts;

*you who chew on hunted fowl and cower before
the very least
of men and women, serfs and slaves, sinners,
serpents, cheats;
why would you be chosen by a king?*

*What arrogance and filthy hope could ever put this
myth inside
your foolish, empty, worthless head; what devil
works so hard to hide
the fact that you were never called, but simply
dreamed, to feed your pride,
the words within the Rings?*

*No king would call a stable boy; less trust him with
a sacred truth!
For who would listen to such a lad: unwashed,
untried, unlearned, uncouth?
Who would listen? Who would see? Where would
be your certain proof
of the words within the Rings?*

*Forget this dream my little child. Hold your
thoughts inside and quiet.
No one need know the blasphemy that took you in*

this darkening night.
For kings and wiser men would speak if there were
truth or even light
in the words within the Rings, dear child.
Leave words within the Rings.

Leave them be and leave them be;
leave them be to fade, to fade.
Leave them be to fade."

With that, the Faereen swept out of the clearing like an ill wind hissing through the trees, and flung the stolen ribbons far into the tangled undergrowth of a deep ravine.

"Self-doubt" it whispered to itself. "Such a powerful curse. So easy."

Ageres woke in the morning and looked out in wonder on the glories of the morning forest. The finest dewdrops reflected the fullness and colours of the early sunshine. Webs of spiders laced themselves across drooping fronds of opening ferns. A tiny squirrel scampered along her path, stopped, stared a question at the boy, and then darted up to the tree-tops to continue on her way.

The world was rich, and his heart was filled with power. He thought of the Message, the Rings. The Rings and the gentle self-evident truth that they held for him. His heart soared. But then, as suddenly, it plummeted. Excitement turned to anxiety.

'What am I doing here, on this strange mission?' he thought. 'Who am I to tell others how to live their lives? What can have possessed me to set out for the Edges, to tell people what, in their hearts, they already know, or choose to ignore?

'What cruel curse has been put on me, that I should pursue this madness? How people would laugh and scorn when I open my mouth to speak. Me, a mere stable boy, presuming to speak of life itself!

'I must return to my duties, bow before my masters and my horses, and seek their forgiveness for my flight to foolishness.'

As soon as his beloved horses came to mind, of course, he thought of Sihdra. She had wandered off, perhaps in search of food. He called her name, but, to his surprise, she did not return.

So he stood, picked up the bridle and carry bag, and walked in search of her. Sometimes the prints of her powerful hooves were clear in the sand. Yet where they came to water, or rock, or tangled scrub, he lost her and had to walk in random circles until, once again, he found her marks.

Finally he saw her, grazing on grasses in a small garden within a hedge of unkempt shrubs. The gate was open, and the grass within the yard was green and long. Behind her there was a remarkable, tiny cottage; old and crooked and tumbledown, but with warm smoke from the chimney, and soft light from its small windows.

"Sihdra!" Ageres called in a loud whisper, not wanting to disturb the occupants of this strange little house. "Sihdra!" The mare did not respond, but stood quietly grazing. The boy was confused; Sihdra never ignored the call of another.

He went closer, trying to keep to the shadows of the trees. "Sihdra! Come. We must return to the City quickly. My masters and your brothers and sisters will see I'm gone, and they will be angry."

But the horse stood, still. The Stableboy moved closer; crept quietly along the muddy path to the gate of the yard, and walked through and up to her. "Sihdra!" he whispered harshly as he bridled her, "It is time to go! We must return to the City." The mare's only response was to glance briefly at him without acknowledgment and drop her great head to the ground once more. But this time, as her head dropped, another appeared behind.

It was an old and wizened face lined with stories;

the hair matted with unkempt age; the eyes piercing and clear. Teeth were missing, and there was straggly down on the chin. It was the face of a woman — a Gnomish woman. Her clothes were a rainbow of rags, and around her neck and arms she wore all manner of stones, strung together in a rattling, clickering, clattering noise.

"Headed for the Edges, I see," said the old woman in a voice that sounded like the crunching of fallen leaves in autumn. The boy's eyes fell to the ground. He was both startled at her in-sight, and embarrassed at his secret exposed.

"I was," he mumbled, knowing he could not hide the truth from a Gnome of such age and knowledge, "but I see I've been foolish and I must return to the City." He began to bridle Sihdra.

"In your foolishness is truth," the woman replied. Gnomes, whose only job is to guard treasures, have no use for formalities and politeness. "The light of the Edges is in your eyes. Do not seek to extinguish it. You are destined to follow it, and follow it you will."

"But I have set out on a fool's quest. I carry high ideas of great truths. Me! A mere Stableboy. I am embarrassed by my arrogance."

Her eyes pierced his, as though striving to reach into his soul.

"Not arrogance, Child. Purpose! Passion! These are what drive you forward. Arrogance might corrupt them to brittle command, but you do not carry arrogance. You carry humility. Humility makes purpose and passion your gift to the world.

"I know little of ideas, and yours are for other places. But I can read hearts, child, as I must to guard treasures. I know noble humility when I see it in the heart. And I know the flame of purpose when I see it in the Spirit. Travel on."

"But old mother, I am no longer sure of my purpose — so how can I be sure of my destination?"

"Sure? No. No-one can be. But turn toward the Edges child, and feel the Spirit flare. And turn towards the City, and feel it flicker and choke away. The Spirit will guide you forward." She said this last as though it were known by all — as though she were saying 'the Sun will rise from the East'. "Follow it. The Edges may not be your destination, but they offer, on this day, your direction. Later, the Spirit may bid you turn away. If it does — again, follow it!"

Ageres could feel truth in the old Gnome's words, and the flame was indeed strong. "I will go, but there is doubt in my heart."

"Haa!!" she screeched, her weathered face alight. "More than doubt, child. Deeper, more powerful than doubt. Confusion! Confusion is all! All that is new pours into your heart. Your courage will not let you hide behind certainty. Let confusion bubble and boil and do its toil. Wisdom will hold you and guide you through tangled pathways. Let confusion be! Let it embrace the doubt. And while confusion does its work, let the Spirit lead. Go!"

Sihdra raised her head, stared expectantly at the boy and whinnied impatiently. Ageres thought no more, but leapt to her back, and bent to whisper in her ear: "To the Edges."

The mare sprang away from the yard like an arrow so that when the boy turned to wave to the old mother Gnome, she and her cottage were lost in the myriad shadows of the forest. He turned forward again, to the wind and the leaves brushing at his hair, the sunshine beaming low through the trees, and to the flame flaring in his heart. "To the Edges," he shouted to the earth and the air. "To the Edges!" And the shout filled the forest and the sky and echoed back to him in the roar of the waterfall and the sigh of the wind and the music of a thousand birdsongs.

And Sihdra galloped forward: obedient, wild and free.

IV

The Emptiness

Together, Ageres and Sihdra travelled on, all that day and the next and a third beyond. The rolling hills of the Higher Fells held many villages. The people there, unlike those in the City, went about their lives steadily and without undue haste. But there was little joy in their step and a weight seemed to press on the shoulders of many. Their eyes were suspicious of this stranger. With a glance they willed him on his way and he, for his part, was pleased to oblige.

Each evening he camped in any inviting glade or field that he could find, and the land fed both him and Sihdra well. Each night the moon would rise a little later, and a little smaller, and the darkness that doused the blazing sunsets grew longer and deeper.

He had, at first, been well pleased that he had chosen this direct route to the Edges, rather than the slower Main Path. They were covering the distance easily. But, as they left the Higher Fells behind, their progress slowed. The Eastern Way dissolved into smaller, forked tracks and he had to use the sun to guide him. On the fourth morning after he had left the mother Gnome's garden, the land was drier, the houses and villages further apart. By afternoon, he could see no signs of human life at all. Leaves underfoot crackled and broke, and the sun shone fiercer. That night, the boy and the mare kept walking until after nightfall in the hope of finding greater nourishment, or human contact. It was a vain hope.

Eventually they stopped and camped by a creek-bed that held no water. What animals or fruit may be in the trees and shrubs were hidden to Ageres's eye. For the first time both he and Sihdra went to sleep with hunger in their bellies. The darkness was yet longer and deeper, so that he could no longer see the trees and distant hills, except as a silhouette of emptiness in the familiar, mysterious star-mist of the sky.

When Ageres woke the next morning the pale, shrinking moon was cowering from the early light of dawn. His hunger was a jagged weight. Sihdra stood as still as rock.

The boy lay still for many minutes, trying not to listen to the niggling trouble that scratched at his heart. Finally, unable to rid himself of the worry, he sat up to stretch his tense muscles, and there, not six paces from him, was an old man, crouching, staring, chewing. His skin was weathered and lined with age. His face was broad, and his eyes were gentle.

"Don't be rushing boy."

Ageres, at first scared, was slightly calmed by the soft voice. Hesitantly, he responded: "I am going to the Edges, old father. I have things to say there. Words that must be heard." His voice stumbled with uncertainty, but the old man seemed not to notice.

"Between you and the Edges is distance and hardship. Don't be rushing. You'll reach your destinations when destiny allows."

With these words, the old man moved quietly through the trees that lined the dry creek bed. He dug at the earth, scratched at bark, lifted fallen branches, and shook low-lying shrubs. Then he made a hole in the dry bed of the river, drew water in a small bark scoop and poured it into a bag of skin.

He came over to Ageres and laid a motley but generous mound of nourishment at his side. Grubs, leaves, tiny berries, seeds and the bag of water.

"Foods of the desert," he said, with reverence. And, as he said it, he gave a slight bow towards the wretched mound, as though in gratitude.

But Ageres did not reach for the food. He was a child of the City. Instead he spoke: "Old father, I am filled with doubts. I am tired and unsure. I am called to the Edges, and a Gnomic mother bid me forward, so what can I do? I must follow. I must!"

"You are tired and unsure. Your body calls for rest and reflection. Listen. Your body is wise. Hardship is ahead of you. You must rest to prepare." His eyes fell once more to the food. "And eat."

"You are kind old father, but these are not the foods I crave. I am more suited to lusher fare. Thank you for your thoughts. But as for nourishment, I will go back to the nearby forests and choose the food that is known to me."

"Then you will not reach the Edges, lad." And he stared straight ahead, looking out toward the eastern horizon.

The Stableboy followed the old man's gaze, and his own eyes widened in fear as he looked into a distance that he had never imagined. The dawn horizon beyond the dry river bed was flat, as though drawn with the finest rule. Around that fine line the colours of earth and sky blended as one into a blazing red as the sun began to rise. For the first time in the boy's life he saw the anger in the sun's early rays — saw a power that might scorch his being, even as, in other places, it softly dried the dew drops from the finest web.

Fear filled his heart. This land was unknown to him. But more than this, he feared his fear, knowing it could turn him away from his quest. The flame still burned, but fear blew at it. If he turned back now the flame, the truth and the passion would be lost, and his journey would crumble, again, to humiliation.

"NO!" he cried. "I will not be turned away. Sihdra, we must go now!" He quickly began to prepare for the ride.

"Wait. Rest. Let me teach you the ways of the Emptiness. You cannot survive alone. Listen to your fear, lad. Listen to your fear and it will guide you. Ignore it and it will haunt you like a ghost that has not been heard. Your fear holds warning. Listen! The way forward will emerge."

"But if I surrender to my fear it will enslave me." Ageres responded, as though with certainty.

"So do not surrender, young man. *Listen*."

Again "NO!" In a rush, he gathered up the food and water that the old man had collected and threw it into the carry bag. Then he jumped to Sihdra's powerful back, and urged the mare eastward.

Momentarily she hesitated. The old man looked on, sad but calm.

"So. It must be so."

These were the last words Ageres heard from him as Sihdra bolted toward the sun.

Within minutes the sweat glistened on Sihdra's coat, and white froth flew to the wind. By mid-morning the heat of the day was fierce though their shadow was still long behind them. Ageres slowed the mare to a canter and then to a walk as they travelled on across that endless void. How far they travelled he could not tell. There were no trees or hills or buildings to mark the distance. The world was sheer emptiness. A great dome of blue met the ground in a simple never-changing circle — an endless floor of red sand and stones, dotted sparsely with dry, sharp-leaved grasses. And not a creature to be seen.

Ageres ate sparingly of the meagre food that the old man had collected, and sipped only a mouthful of the water at a time. Yet still, at the end of the second day, the food and water were gone. He had offered both to Sihdra but she refused, chewing, instead, on the wretched plants that clung low to the desert floor.

On the third morning, hope visited him briefly. He saw, ahead, a strange city of thin houses; welcome structures against the endless blue sky. But as they neared these structures, his heart was struck low once again. They were nothing but gnarled towers of earth, as though the desert floor had spat its sand angrily toward the sky, only to have it frozen in punishment.

Frustrated, Ageres kicked at one of the towers, breaking the edges, only to reveal that it was made by the tiniest of ants, alive with industry and busy-ness. These creatures were thriving in this place of death, and the Stableboy, in his desperate weakness, hated them for it.

Another day on he was near defeat. Death and hopelessness seemed upon him. He had been walking alongside Sihdra, hoping to conserve the energy of the flagging mare, but now he could walk no more. His Spirit was struck low and his body had no nourishment to move it forward. He used his last strength to climb on to the loyal mare's back, and slumped forward as though unconscious: parched, weak and helpless.

The line between thoughts and dreams, reality and illusion, was lost. His mind blurred and distorted the barren world around him and the rings of the Message floated and swirled through his head. He tried to focus on them to find safety, but instead felt taunted by them. One of the rings became the whole horizon — this circle of death that he was in. Another began to shrink, tightening around his throat so that he could not speak. Another grasped tight around his chest so that he could not breathe, and another gripped his hands so that he could not save or feed himself. The colours of the overlapping rings mixed and faded and baked to pale until there was only the red of the earth and the blue of the sky, and his body and clothing were melting to the red of the earth and the blue of the sky, as though he was becoming one with them.

He began to sense, in this terrible infinite silence, that this is how it must be. Finally he resigned himself to the blue and the red and wanted only to be a part of them. He wanted to tell Sihdra to leave him here and go on alone, but he had no voice. He opened his eyes to pull at the horse's mane but, as he did so, he realised that Sihdra had stopped. "Thank you, dear friend," he mouthed, readying to slip his body to its final rest. "Go well. If you find the world once again, think of my Spirit." With that, he made one last effort and threw himself to the ground. But he was shocked to find himself face down in coolness and liquid and soft mud. It got into his gut and he coughed and spluttered and choked and laughed and looked up at Sihdra with wide, delighted, confused eyes.

Though his sight was blurred, he could see that he lay at the edge of a small, shallow, muddy water hole. Around it were low, thin trees that shaded the ground and offered life once again. He drank. And, as the shadows of the day grew long, he slept where he lay in the damp mud; slept so deep that he might not have existed for that whole evening and night. When he woke in the morning and searched his memory the night was but a deep, dark nothingness. And in the lee of that nothingness he felt, briefly, whole.

That morning, more good fortune befell him. A small lizard came to drink at the waterhole. The boy lay still, watching it. Then slowly, carefully, noiselessly, he brought himself up to his haunches and, when the lizard moved into the water, he sprang, grabbed the poor creature, and broke its neck with a single flick of his hand, just as he had seen his grandfather do on outings beyond the city bounds. Such was his hunger that he immediately bit at the belly of the dead lizard, chewing greedily at the flesh that lay beneath the cool skin. He offered no prayer, nor thanks.

For an hour more he rested and hoped for more game to arrive, but none came. Worse, he saw from the stains in the sand that the waterhole was growing rapidly smaller. He was going to have to move from this place within days. It offered only temporary reprieve from the Emptiness. But he was still exhausted, and fell to a fitful sleep. Again, he dreamed of the Rings. But they were still in disarray.

When he woke, the sun was high, and his mind was clearer. He knew he had to gather himself, and tried to order his thoughts. 'I have come by a great Message, and yet feel lost. Perhaps, if I look more carefully, I will find guidance within its rings. Perhaps the rings might lead me out of this silent Emptiness.' He drew the beautiful symmetry of the Message in the sand and searched for its answers. There were the four points of the compass. And each point of the compass pointed, in turn, to three rings of a trinity. Could the centre-point of each Ring be just the guidance he needed? Having nothing else to guide him, he concluded that it must be so.

He drew lines from the Centre of the message to two centre-points of each Trinity, and then to the third, so that the lines formed a long diamond to the East, and then the North, and then the South.

These diamond lines, he decided, might form the paths he should follow in search of nourishment and safety. The geometric beauty of the plan convinced him that it must be right. He filled his leather bag with water and set off with Sihdra once again.

For three days he rode south of east, and around the horizon, and back from the north of east. He found nothing but emptiness.

For three days he rode northward in the same

way and around and back, and another three days towards the south. Still, he found nothing but emptiness.

Between his journeys to the east and the north and the south he drank water from the ever shrinking waterhole, and he waited for more creatures to appear, but none came.

On his twelfth evening in the desert, when no moon graced the night, the waterhole was dry. The certainty — that had driven him to follow the imagined lines of his message to the east and south and north — was broken. Once again, he gave in to the power of this vast Emptiness; once again felt himself melting to the red of the earth and the blue of the skies. As he drifted towards sleep, he felt his smallness; felt at one with the tiny ants and the scattered blades of grass. Yet in the next moment he felt himself boundless, un-constrained; his Spirit afloat across the desert and the endless star-filled sky.

He felt like he was being called home, but did not yet know where home was.

Finally the darkness of a dreamless, endless sleep was upon him.

Yet, come morning, he woke. Gradually he recognised, in his waking, the voice of the old man who had bid him rest, chanting high and rhythmic.

Little brother, little brother, let the dreaming now return.

Let the stars shine on your heart and let the flame inside you burn.

Let the breezes of the sky and the earth of sand and stone

become once more a part of you, and be no more alone.

Little brother, little brother, let the waking now begin.

Let the tree within you sway and let the bird within you sing.

Let the sun within you rise and the river in you flow

to the places you belong to, where the Spirit longs to go.

Over and over the old man chanted his song, so that Ageres, as he slowly surfaced towards consciousness, felt like he had been listening to it forever, yet only now begun to hear.

Finally he sat up and looked to the old man. But this time he was deeply grateful to see him crouching, staring, and chanting slow and high.

When he saw Ageres rise, the old man stood up from his haunches and walked a few paces this way, a few paces that. He reached into some spindly grass, dug at some barren sand, turned some useless rocks and presented Ageres, once again, with a mound of food and a gourd of water. Once again he graced it with a small bow of gratitude. Food had never tasted so good to the starving Stableboy.

He ate gratefully as the old man dug deeper into the damp sand, drawing water for Sihdra's thirst. When that was done, the old man rested, and waited.

They sat in silence for what may have been minutes; may have been hours. Ageres knew only that he was alive, and that life called him again.

Finally, he found words.

"Old father, I am grateful. This land is cruel, and chooses death before life."

"No, child. This land is generous if we choose life within it."

"But father, I brought great knowledge to it. Yet even then, the land would not respond!"

The old man gazed at the horizon. "It is hard to listen when your heart is haunted by fear and death.

This land chooses life in many forms. The Emptiness is rich when you learn to listen to its silence. It holds nourishment, but the songs that will lead you there are sung in whispers."

Ageres felt that the strange man had not yet understood him. But he did not have the strength to explain, and said nothing.

In response to his silence, the old man stood. He began to sing to himself and set off toward the horizon. The Stableboy and the mare, having no alternative but death, chose to follow.

Day after day they wandered the Emptiness together. The lad did not ride the mare, for she had been weakened by thirst, and the pace of the old man was slow and patient. Their journey took them in all directions and the boy could not discern any sense in their path, except that his stomach was not empty and his throat was not dry. Every day the colours were of ochre and blue and yet, as he began to know the Emptiness, he could see its vividness and endless variety. The world changed shape many times, from unending flatness to sharp cracked mountains.

Sometimes, the old man led them to the shade of jagged cliffs; to cool dank places of mud and moisture with mosses and lichen that seemed, to the boy, like the most glorious forest. There, he would strip himself naked and roll gratefully in the wet, dark mud and suck at the mosses. And afterwards he would lay on his back, still naked and trusting and open to the sky.

He reveled in the dirt and the moisture. It somehow brought him closer to the soul of this vast Emptiness. And it brought him closer to rich and mysterious places within him that he could not name.

Gradually Ageres began to see, even in the most barren parts of the Emptiness, not desert but garden. The old man gathered plants and insects, grubs and water as though they were placed for his taking. Some he cooked on fire. Some he crushed and baked in the sun or pasted with water. Some he offered straight from the shrubs.

Ageres marvelled at the old man's ability to find so much nourishment in such a place when he himself — with a City schooling and the deep truth of the Message that he had found — had almost starved.

One night he tried to explain his Message to the old man. "I have been shown signs of great truth. Yet here in the Emptiness, they failed me." He drew the Message in the sand. He drew the four compass points, and then the twelve rings around and their words, revealing the flower of truth that shone in his heart. Then he explained how he had used the shape of the rings to guide his search from the waterhole, out and around the east and south and north.

The old man smiled, then chuckled. He looked at the Stableboy, then at the Rings he had drawn, then at the horizon, and back again to the lad's message and his whole body erupted into laughter that brought tears to his eyes.

But after a while his laughter subsided, and he looked again at Ageres and saw that he was confused and hurt. The old man spoke gently, though still smiling. "Your message is not for this place."

There was silence for a while. But then he went on, carefully. "These are good rings and words lad. But they cannot guide you in the Emptiness." He waved his hand in slow silent circles, as if describing the vastness around. "The pathways of the Emptiness are found in songs and poems that are whispered in breezes; hidden in sand. You cannot plan your way, and the paths and maps of others will not guide you." He paused, as though leaving space for the Stableboy to understand. "But if you listen to the Emptiness, if you love its harshness, if you give thanks for its gifts, it will treat you well. And you will hear, in the silence, the small, quiet voice that guides you."

The Stableboy heard his words, and did not speak again that night.

Over the days and nights that followed, the simple, vivid lines of the desert and the confident colours, so few in number and so strong in depth, drew Ageres into the soul of the Emptiness, and washed him clean.

The moon grew slowly full again, and again slowly disappeared. The old man said little, so that sometimes it was as though he was simply a mirage; an imagining that the young man held in his heart.

On the twenty-eighth dawn of their wanderings, as light crept over the moonless sky, the old man stared into Ageres's eyes longer than he ever had before. "Today you return to places of things and structures. Destinations will lead you once more. But remember these days and this place, lad. Keep the whispered songs of the Emptiness in your heart."

They walked east, and a blue escarpment slowly rose out of the flat red Emptiness. As they approached, Ageres could see that the way ahead was walled by massive cliffs, seemingly impassable. He felt fear again. Was his journey from the Emptiness to be blocked by these towering walls? But as they drew closer he noticed a thin splinter of light in the cliff face. Slowly it revealed itself as a deep, narrow chasm through the escarpment.

At the far end of the chasm, not a thousand paces distant, the boy could glimpse rolling hills dotted with trees and shrubs. On a distant hillside, miraculously, a small low fence marked the landscape, separating it, one side from the other.

His heart filled with the welcoming pleasure of homecoming. Soon he would be, again, amongst women and men, marked paths and gates, buildings and fields and fences. Soon he would be, again, in a world that was familiar to him.

But there was sadness, too, in this homecoming. He wondered: in amongst the crowds and the structures, would he still hear the beautiful whispered songs of the Emptiness?

He turned to share his jumbled feelings with the old man. But he was gone.

Ageres stared back for one last time at the simple beauty of the desert, yearning for its quiet simplicity, even as he yearned for the destinations of lusher lands. He thought back on his forty days there; thought back to the twelve days of death and the twenty-eight of whispered songs and random beauty, and he saw that they had opened new parts of him. He sensed, also, that they had left his Spirit silent and waiting, ready to be re-enchanted with new awakenings.

His reverie was broken by Sihdra, who whinnied softly. Together, they walked through the narrow, shaded chasm that formed their gateway from the Emptiness to the Edges.

The floor of the chasm was as stony and sandy as the desert, and as flat. But the boy stared up in awe at the towering walls. He felt the coolness of their shade as though it was a deep pool. He listened to the echo of his footsteps and breathing, and the rustle of his clothes. His time in the Emptiness had made his senses sharp and grateful; he experienced this simple, narrow world in its full glory, and surged on and through to find more.

Eventually the cliff walls lowered and opened to a world of low hills with trees for shade and berries for food, and a dry creek bed that would, he knew, show him the way to the Edges, for they lay near the Ocean. And creeks and streams — even dry ones — must find their way, in time, to the Ocean.

Before the sun was low he had reached a place where the creek bed, still dry, crossed over a small rock-face. At the base was a pool; dark and deep. He threw himself in carelessly and splashed with glee. Every droplet on his body was a sweet caress.

Sihdra drank heartily from the pool, and watched her Stableboy with a patient eye.

There was still light in the day, and they could have travelled on. But Ageres was so enchanted and comforted by the still, deep, generous water that he rested by it, swam in it and drank from it through the afternoon and the evening and the night.

V

The Edges

Ageres and Sihdra woke before the dawn and were soon on their way, continuing to follow the small creek bed that had led them out of the Emptiness. At first the creek seemed to hold its water beneath the sand, and in occasional pools. As they walked on, though, a small trickle emerged and stayed constant. By noon it was a dancing brook, by mid-afternoon an eddying stream, and, just before nightfall, it joined with a swirling, flowing river. Alongside the river was a rutted, well-used track. Again the boy camped, this time soothed by the sound of flowing water.

At first light he was woken by the sound of voices. It was the high musical lilt of the Edgelings. Of course Ageres had seen Edgelings before. They came to the City often in those days. Sometimes they came to speak with the King and his advisers about the Edges and their well-being. Sometimes they came to barter and trade. Well known as a spirited people, they bowed to no-one and were greeted by most City folk and Central Uplanders with a touch of fear.

There was much laughter and fire in them, and they were rarely silent. They made their own entertainment, though most in the City felt that it was of a sort that no civilised person would join in. There was anger in them too. For the Kingdom had not always treated them well.

The Edgelings whose voices woke him that morning were typically tall and dressed in wild and wayward clothes of clashing colours. He was struck, after the gentleness of the old father of the Emptiness, by the fire and sharpness of their voices and the skip and dance in their gait. He sat up as they passed and stared at their backs as they tripped and weaved their way along the track.

Suddenly though, he heard another approaching him and he turned to see her; angular and thin and full of spring in her step.

She seemed shocked to see him, but also pleased. "Now what and which and what again would a City boy be doing here, dossed down all doefully and doddle-eyed in the uplands of the Edges? Where have you come from lad we wonder and worry and wander about?"

"I have come from the City, madam." Ageres replied tentatively.

"No madam, child, but Lemma. And I am not blind or batty or blunt, sweet citified sir, so I can see with an eye diddle diddle that the City's in you and never will leave. But how did you reach this very right now and right about here spot? And why, I'm wondering, why?"

Ageres struggled, at first, to follow her dancing, playful language. She strung words together like so many coloured beads; paid no mind, in her speaking, to rules and order. She spoke as though language itself were a game or a pastime. That was the way with Edgelings.

But once he had understood her question he responded.

"I came through the Emptiness. I came because I have a Message that must be spoken, and I feel that only the Edgelings can hear."

The woman sparkled and laughed. "Well it's long ago and far away since a Civic sought to confound and astound, and riddle me riddle me re. So I retire and yield and fall down dead; what mean you by 'the Emptiness'?"

"It is a great dry place, with no water and no food to see, unless you know the hiding places of darkness and shadow and dust."

For the first time the woman's brow creased. "The Plain of Fire? You tell me, and lead me and hope that I heed thee that you have crossed the Plain of Fire without the waters of winter? Sir of the baffling and boring, I love a riddle but I hate a lie. So tell me the honest and nothing-but truth. Where do you come from? Where do you go?"

"Good woman, I would not lie. I have come across the Emptiness. I was guided and fed by a wise and kind old father, who led me to a great chasm and I have followed the stream of that chasm to this very place."

"Goodnessly graciously mercifully me. I have heard tall tales and few of the old men of the Fire. Let me see your deepest eyes, lad. Is this the truth?"

"The truth, on the life of the King."

"Well that would not be a long-live-the-lollipop sort of promisey pledge around here, but I know for you City folk it tells of the truth. So, amazed and re-phrased let me ask in refrain — why and why and why again?"

"I have a Message in me, and I have come to the Edges to speak it, for only here will people hear."

"The lad puns at least, but speaks not a word of sensible serious sanity. What message from a City boy would we wild and woolly Edgelings seek, except perhaps some news of your ever-changing tyrannical toys?"

Ageres, suddenly shamed, looked at the ground. "Good woman, I have tried to hide that question in the pit of my stomach for my entire journey. All I know is that I have had a fire in my heart that leads me to the Edges, and bids me carry my truth. I hope the Message will have the power to overcome my fears, and your cynicism."

"Well truth to tell and tell it square, we Edgelings are not ones for listening. We go about our business with a laugh and giggle, and we let the world drift by. Hard to say, even for a wild and wily Edgeling, but I think you came through the Plains of Fire for wastily, nothingly, emptily nil. Still, join me on my meandering way and bring your farting and fur coated friend, and I will show you giggles and sights. You shall have skittles and cheer after your great ordeal. By the time we part, your message will be a lot of old letters, free adrift on the wind."

With a heavy heart, the young man stood and walked on with the bright, babbling woman. He wondered, again, what had made him think that his Message should be told.

As they walked along the track they saw other Edgelings making their way. Ageres noticed that his companion did not greet them. Instead, she kept her gaze from theirs, and afterwards whispered harsh words to him, providing him with a list of their failings.

"She there wears the clashing, clumsical clothes of the vile village of Arrogere. Full they are of their own uppity muppity self-importantlies."

And of another: "That man there with his eyes to the hoity-toity heavenses is said and said and said again to be rather too frolicking friggingly friendly with those of four legs and too little brain."

And of a child: "Look at that child, now; poor little mite of a mouse. What fault his that he's born to a mother who will not keep him, a father who does not know him? Some people are simply too me and me mean to deserve the love of a child."

The boy was puzzled at her venom, and finally his puzzlement found voice. "Good woman — Lemma — I have heard that the Edgelings are a spirited people, and when they come to the City they seem united indeed. But now I see suspicion and separation. Must you all live in fear of each other?"

"Well puzzle me over and call me queen, what sort of question is that? I fear no other! Life is a giggle and a gift indeed, but you mustn't deny that most of the world is made up of the foul, the foolish, and the failures. I live with good people, and they're enough for me. I don't need to go bowing down worshiply to any old fool that I find on the road."

"But I see bitterness in your heart."

Lemma stopped; tightened. After a silence she spoke. Her playful language disappeared. Her tone was hard and cold and flat: "What bitterness is there, child, is mine to do with what I will. Now you keep your eyes on the track, and out of my heart." Her face had gone dark, and she did not speak for many a turn in the path. Ageres knew he had caused offence, crossing into territory where he was not invited. So he, too, held his silence. And in his silence, his attention slowly turned to the country they were walking through.

Their path followed a broad valley, crossing from one side to the other and back again. The stream at the base of the valley cut deep into the earth, forming small canyons of crystal and magic. Several times the Stableboy paused in wonder at the stream's journey through these canyons. He felt cleansed by its beauty. Water danced down carved rock, now pausing in still pools, now spraying fountains and shards of light. It played gently with whatever obstacles were placed in its path, skipping and turning, waiting and gathering, then letting go for long silver dream-like falls. And all the way the stream sang and skipped, so that the strange and difficult rock of the valley seemed hand carved for the water's journey to the sea.

But the spell that the valley was casting on him was soon and suddenly broken. As Lemma was leading him over a ridge that stood at a curve in the river he came to a terrible sight. The glorious forest that they had been walking through suddenly gave way to a carnage of scarred timber and wasted ground.

"Good woman, what have your people done?"

Lemma's anger erupted: "My people, boy? *My* people? These trees fall to the hunger of City houses and City fire and City paper for your fancy City words. This land was long ago won by you Civics, and is not ours to control. The Civic hunger is never sated. It has eaten your own trees. It has eaten the trees of the Uplands and Midlands. And now it reaches the Edges."

Ageres was shaken by her anger, but felt compelled to challenge this carnage. "But you could stop this. This land could be used for food or nourishment for your people. It is Edgelings who cut the forest, Edgelings who take their wages. It is Edgelings who destroy the magic just to get the money of the City! You have the power to simply stop!" His young face was flushed and defiant.

Suddenly, the woman sat down. She looked tired, but she held Ageres with her stare; honest and fierce.

"Listen, lad. The world changes. You in the City see the changes every day. You create and embrace the changes. They excite you. But you think that because we Edgelings still live close to the earth and the oceans and the forests, because we still talk in spirited tongue, because we still speak of strangeness and magic, our world is not changing.

"Our visits to the City entertain you. And our forests keep you warm. Yet you do not see our changes or our pain. It is always so with the Civilised Civics. The City draws from the Edges, yet ignores our needs."

Lemma stared around at the stumps and debris of the shattered forest.

"You can see: our world is being slowly eaten by the City's demands and the Edges' compliance." Then she glared back at Ageres. "Look to your own when you speak of this damage. How can we stand against those who ignore the very soul of their living and their Kingdom? Those who ignore soul will always ignore the Edges; will always turn away from the essence of their world.

"The fish from the ocean, the grains from the land, the timber from the forests are all growing thin. And *still* you call for more fish, more grain, more timber — carelessly ignoring the ocean, the land, the forests.

"These, lad, are the soul and the nourishment that you Civics so sorely need, but you turn away. You call for more of the parts, but you ignore the whole; you call for more of the 'things' but you ignore the soul.

"You strive madly toward destruction. And we get drawn towards the madness. Some Edgelings visit the City and try to make you see — a foolish quest if ever there was one. And as the riches of the ocean and of the land and of the forests are reduced to scraps, so the strong bonds of the Edgelings turn to constant, petty quarrel. Our Spirit is choked away. And who can wonder, boy. Who can wonder?

"The world changes. The Edges suffer; but you Civics will not see it. The soul suffers; but you Civics will not feel it."

She paused in her angry speech, and gathered her things together as though to walk on. But then she looked to the path ahead, and back at the Stableboy, and then to the ground. And she sighed.

"Yes, lad, the challenge in your eyes is true. We accept the money of the City and so have changed our ways. Now we yearn for the subsistence that feeds our soul, even as we grasp for the money that feeds our greed. We Edgelings could respond to the changes. We could again begin to build new ways of living. We could stand against the ignorant pillage. But the world changes too fast. We are tired and weary, and we fight and bicker, and our soul thins, just as yours does.

"I do not know the answer. But I must live on. And so I do what must be done. See those blue hills ahead, that look so serene and mysterious from here? They are littered with broken trees. I have done that.

With others of my village, I have stolen the trees from the land around us; stolen them in exchange for the money that the City provides. I must live on. So I do what the City demands. It is wrong, but the world changes, and it is the only way forward I know."

Her eyes moistened, and she turned to hide them.

Ageres had been averting his gaze to the damp moss-covered rocks that lined their pathway. When she was done, he sat in silence, and did not lift his eyes. Finally he spoke. "I have much to learn of the world. I carry a Message — a Message of answers. Yet, as I travel, I just find more questions."

"Ah my churlishly cheekily chuffable child, don't hang your hairy head so. You may not know the curly questions, but your ears are open, and your heart is a hero — it never turns away. Let's walk and talk and stalk horizons, and let our hearts giggle again."

And with that she sprang to her feet and resumed her journey toward her blue, beautiful hills with the scars still hidden to the boy's eyes, but now known to his heart. For his part, Ageres was happy to hear the song return to Lemma's words, and he jumped up to walk beside her on the path.

As they passed by villages and people she resumed her happy, hard-edged tirade against all and sundry, playing games with her words once again. Ageres let the words float past him, and turned his mind to the breeze on his face, and the sun on his back, and the narrow, winding path at his feet.

The Stableboy spent that night in the common-house of Lemma's village, warmed by the dance of lamplight and shadows. He wondered, yet again, why he had felt driven to the Edges to deliver his Message, for it seemed clear that his words and rings would hold no interest for these villagers. But he did not dwell on this. He simply let himself be amongst them, laughing and crying at the tall and hilarious tales that they told. Tales of the misdeeds of half-known fools; tales of the brave and noble work of his hosts in standing against the ignorance and incompetence of the strangers of their world. He knew the stories belied the Kingdom's rich diversity, but saw, also, that his own certainty had done the same, and so he held his silence.

In the morning he rose early with excitement, for the villagers had told him that he was less than a day's walk from the legendary 'ocean' of childhood stories. Lemma walked him to the gate to bid him farewell, babbling away in her darting, swirling tongue, and forced cheeriness. At the gate she held his gaze as if to be sure he was listening. "Young Ageres — pay no mind to my quips and quibbles. Quest on and question, lad, and your message and meaning will find its place."

With that she slapped him gently on the arm, and turned and danced up the path like a leaf blowing in the wind, and did not look back.

Ageres mounted Sihdra and they rode on.

VI

The Ocean

The track that they followed continued to wind with the river, but the river slowly changed its nature, growing wider, calmer and less hurried.

Around mid-morning, Ageres could hear a faint sigh ahead. Gradually, as he and Sihdra walked on, the sigh grew to a roar. Then, as they rounded a bend, the water and the valley simply disappeared, falling over the edge of a great escarpment. His eye, though, was carried beyond the edge; on to the distance. There he saw the ocean that he had heard so much about, yet, he realised now, had never fully imagined. It was blue like the sky, and the line between the two may have been mere fancy. A million sparks played on its surface as it reflected the sun. It seemed lifeless, and yet alive with deep, constant, glorious movement as wind and wave and mystery played across it.

For long minutes his Spirit was lost in confusion and joy and wonder. He sat on a rock and stared gratefully at the sight and explored his thoughts, finally speaking them to the patient Sihdra. "Friend, I began this journey with an answer to my questions. Yet all I find is how much more there is to know."

He was learning: the journey to truth is rich indeed. It is not marked by more facts, but by deeper mystery.

Filled with the excitement of it, he stood and walked right to the edge of the precipice by the waterfall, and shouted joyously at the ocean like a fool, or a messenger: "I have riches, unseen! I have riches, unheard! I have riches unknown!" Then he turned, ran at Sihdra and leapt to her back and they sprang forward together in a joyous gallop.

The path led down the face of the rough escarpment and followed the river in its final journey to the Ocean. Soon they were riding through the simple fishing village that nested at the river's mouth. But Ageres barely noticed the surprised faces of the Seafarers who lived there, and paid them no mind as he urged the mare into the cold salty water. His delighted laughter rang through the air, and Sihdra's soft whinnying sang with the sound of the waves lapping and the pebbles knocking together, and the solitary cry of a gull on the wing.

Ageres swam and splashed and frolicked in the surf until his fingers began to wrinkle, and he was shivering with cold. Only as he emerged from the water's edge did he realise that a crowd of Seafarers had gathered together on the launching ground next to the brightly coloured boats that took them to sea; gathered together to stare.

He had never met Seafarers before, though he knew of them. They were few in number, scattered in small villages along the Ocean's edge. For Ageres, as for most, they were people of mystery. They seemed uninterested in the ways and workings of the Kingdom, and few visited the City. They gave their attention to the Ocean.

Like the Edgelings, they had their own way with words, but here, now, they seemed silenced by his presence, and by the great mare that stood beside him.

Ageres walked towards them nervously, dripping the ocean's water to the sand. The clothes of the Seafarers were faded and few — baggy, tattered shorts, and roughly woven hessian tops that covered their shoulders, but left their arms to move free.

Finally, a young woman found voice. "I's sorry good Civic for us' stares and mumblings. It's not many Civics is swimming round here. Me's aunties and uncles and cousins and sisters is not feeling easy with strangers and fears."

"Be hushed now young miss!" spoke another — far older, worn and wizened. "No apologisings is needed, but guidance — for himself to find he's way."

Both women spoke in a swirling, lilting melody that was, to the ear, what the flight of the swallow is to the eye.

The old woman spoke again, this time direct to Ageres. "So young himself, talk and ask of destinations, and us' guidance will get you closer there."

"But sea woman — I believe that I have arrived. For I bring a Message that must be heard. And I have been driven to the Edges to tell it. So please, listen to the truth of three Rings and seven. Twelve and twenty-eight."

Immediately, he picked up a small piece of driftwood, and began to draw the Rings in the packed sand of the launching ground. With passion, he began to deliver this Message that he had come to love so much. With passion, but also urgency; perhaps fear. For in the deep memory that had no name, he knew that he was driven to take his Message to the Edges. And there was no further to go. Beyond this was merely ocean, and empty horizons. If the Message were not delivered here, then where? This was his fear.

Above his fear, though, his passion for the Rings remained unwavering, and he spoke on.

Yet no sooner had he begun to speak than people began to wander away, a glazed look of disinterest in their eyes.

"Good people! Stay! It is only in their fullness —
in the twelve and the twenty-eight — that you can see
their beauty. Stay and you will know truth!"

But another, and then another of the small crowd
moved away until just a young man remained, only a
few years older than Ageres. His clothes were faded
to pastel, and his eyes were the grey of a dolphin. To
look at him was to see the sea spray on the pounding
waves; the endless light clouds on the winds.

He was clearly a Seafarer, but, to Ageres's surprise,
he spoke in the dialect of the City. "Don't think them
rude," he said to Ageres. "Words and geometry are
not their language. They cannot feel passion for these
things."

"But these are not just words and geometry,"
snapped the Stableboy. "These are of the Spirit! You
Seafarers are famous for your Spirit. I offer you words
to give that Spirit voice!"

"Thank you, sir, but we respectfully decline.
There are more voices in the sea and the sky than
were ever in the throats of humans. And they need
not speak in words."

"But I have been driven to the Edges. I know that
you must hear. I have felt a flame within me that has
driven me to this place, to your village, to the edge
of the land, where the ocean begins. I know that you

must hear. And yet you greet me with apathy and call it deafness! Of course words are your language, just as they are mine. Do not feign deafness just to give comfort to your ignorance!"

Although Ageres's certainty angered the Seafarer, his eyes and voice and words stayed calm and steady. Calm and steady, but strong — like a brewing storm. "I feign no ignorance, nor deafness, nor do I speak of apathy. Have you seen the sleeping power and beauty of the ocean on an early spring day? Have you heard the song of the whale, or seen the glistening dance of the dolphin? Have you felt the rage and disdain of a winter's storm at sea, or felt the gift of a sparkling fish, pulled from the depths for your food? If not, boy, do not speak to me of ignorance; do not speak to me of deafness."

Ageres, still angry himself, was yet mute in the face of this simmering tirade.

"And some among that crowd that you drove away with your preaching have seen and heard even more. They have dived beneath the sparkling waters to find a world unknown, filled with creatures that you cannot even imagine. They have found a world of weightlessness, where every plant and creature is engaged in a glorious slow, synchronised dance. And they have dived into the blue darkness, where the human eye can only dimly see, and whose mystery gives the light of dry land a special meaning.

"A few, even, have faced the fire and terror of dragons that can burn to the human soul; have cowered in their boats as those wild monsters swoop upon them with their wings blocking the sun; have even tamed the terrifying creatures in the only way known — to stare into their eyes and call them brother, call them sister, call them self.

"Do not call us ignorant, boy, until you have known these things, and have let them into your heart. But then you would not call us ignorant. You would call us friend. And you would speak our language."

His anger, with his last words, subsided, and compassion returned. His piercing gaze, that had held Ageres silent, softened, and he spoke again. "I see the passion your rings create in you. It is good, and powerful. But if you invite the audience of others, and they have no need to hear, let them go their way. Otherwise your gift becomes a tyranny, your truth becomes merely a chain.

"We Seafarers embrace the mystery. Your rings speak of explanations. These are of little use to us. They may be of use to others. But they are of little use to us."

Ageres was confused. Finally, he spoke. "It seems that my quest is merely a chase between false horizons. Perhaps the flame has driven me to the Edges in order to make me see my own stupidity; to rid me of any notions that I should quest for more than shit and straw."

"Ah friend. Cheer up. You will find your way in good time. Meanwhile, walk with me along the beach and I will tell you tales of the Seafarers. I am called Mustes. What do they call you?" Ageres told him, and together they went to the water's edge and turned to walk along the jagged coast.

Sihdra walked quietly for a while, but it was not long before the grandeur, the endlessness and the purity of the ocean-side had sung to the wildness within her. Ageres, sensing the cry of freedom, removed her ropes, and lay them over his shoulder. Un-bridled, she surged on ahead, kicking and rearing, prancing and galloping until she seemed to disappear into the myriad colours of cliffs and sand, water and waves, clouds and gulls and sky.

Ageres and Mustes spoke as they walked, slowly revealing and connecting to an easier rhythm. Mustes gradually allowed the melodies of his Seafarer's dialect to re-emerge, and Ageres felt the rich rhythm of it, as though it were part of the waves and the floating clouds.

Mustes told him, briefly, of his own life. He had sought out education and opportunity in the City and spoke fondly of his time there, but also of his yearning for the Ocean. "I's loving the knowledge, and loving the mystery, and yearning for both. Yourselves in the City does too much forgetting for I, but I like yous' inventing. So I's living at the sea to remember the mystery, and I's visit the City to learn of the new."

Ageres asked him to speak of the ocean and Mustes happily obliged.

He told tales of dragons and sea serpents, of the migration of birds and the places they see, of lands that have no name and the people that visit from them; of treasures known but never reached in submerged caves. He spoke of waves the size of mountains; of shells as delicate as snowflakes and, with love in his voice, of the quiet dance of the world beneath the water that tempts people to stay below when their lungs are fit to burst.

Ageres could not tell which stories were real and which were from imaginings, but they eased his pain and he was grateful for the company.

As they walked, he saw all manner of beauty. The silver lines that the waves left behind on the sand; the pebbles that had been smoothed and polished for all time; the curve and flurry of the sea-birds' flight; the gnarled, swirling lines of the cliffs — as though the rock itself had been bent and twisted by some mysterious and glorious force. As the sun dropped behind the cliff's face the beach came to an end, where a rocky headland jutted out into the sea. Sihdra stood waiting for them there, and they stopped to watch the spray of waves as they crashed against the rocks. Ageres looked to his feet, and picked up a tiny, gleaming, spiral shell. He rolled it between his fingers, and stared at it in different lights. "If all of creation had conspired only to form the perfection of this shell," he said — speaking to himself and the ocean as much as to Mustes — "it would have been time well spent."

Mustes smiled silently and nodded. Then, after a pause, he said "Time is calling for ourselves' returning."

"I think I will stay a while," Ageres announced, and Mustes made no protest, even though the shadows of the cliffs stretched long in the lowering sun.

"As yourself likes. A deep cave lies waiting within thems cliffs. Seafarers sometimes visits it for solitude and wonderings. It gives shelter from the wind and cold, and a high dry platform, carved smooth for the sleep. There's food in the rock-pools around. The Mare can find feed and high ground in the shrubbery above the beach."

He paused, stared at the ocean, then back at Ageres. "I will bid yourself farewell, Ageres. I's hoping the message will find its place of meaning." He paused, staring openly into Ageres's eyes as though searching for something deep within. "Yourself has a heart that is true. The soul is waiting."

They shook hands as friends, and the Seafarer turned and moved into a slow trot, down to the water's edge and along through the shallows, returning to his home.

With his companion gone Ageres, who had wanted time to reflect, suddenly felt deeply troubled. He was sad and alone, and his confusion was tangled within him. He swam once again, and felt the gentle power of the sea lift and move his body as though he were in flight, and knew that he did not understand it.

He climbed on to the wet rocks and looked down into the world of magic and strangeness beneath the surface, and knew that he did not understand it.

He walked back onto the beach where the damp skin of his legs picked up countless tiny grains of sand, all carved from the majesty of the rocks, or the fragility of the shells — carved through millennia unknown — and knew that he did not understand any of it.

Because he could not know what plants and creatures in this mysterious world were safe to eat, he dared eat none. So as the skies darkened he crawled — cold, confused and hungry — into the depths of the cave that Mustes had pointed to, leaving Sihdra grazing above the beach. He felt for the smooth platform of rock that Mustes had spoken of, climbed to it, and sought the sanctuary of sleep.

As he lay on the platform, his eyes were open but un-seeing in the dark. He was — deeply — confused. What had led him to pursue this strange quest? What was he doing alone in this cave, at the very edge of his known world? He retraced the long, strange journey in his mind. He could remember the powerful feelings of truth and destiny that had driven him across the Dawn Pass towards the Edges. But he also recalled how foolish he had felt on waking the next morning. The Message of truth in his heart had been, still, bright and strong. But he had remembered, that morning — he was only a Stableboy.

That was the power of the Faereen's curse. But Ageres, of course, did not know that.

Why had he listened to the Gnomic woman's urgings? He had almost died in the Emptiness, saved only by the Old Man's whispered songs. And then his doubts had been proved right: the Edgelings and Seafarers were not interested in his truth; not interested in his words and rings. And he was still feeling stung by Mustes's angry rejection of his certainty.

So he could only conclude, in the darkness: 'The Gnomic woman, surely, was wrong. The fire within, which drove me toward the Edges, was no more than a trick of the heart to justify my travels. Now the trick is revealed. My confusion and foolishness are complete. I must return to the City, to the stable, to my destiny of shit and straw.'

He tried to console himself, and to ease the heaviness that he felt, by speaking aloud into the darkness: "Ah well — I will always have the journey to look back on. And I have the Message; I have the Rings. At least I have found them."

Sadly placated by these words, he finally drifted into a fitful sleep.

The Stableboy had also found wisdom.
But he did not know that then.

He woke to a strange new sound. The cave had become waist deep in gently rippling water that lapped and sang against its walls. The ocean had risen beyond his imaginings or understanding. He was amazed. He had heard tales of how the oceans breathed in this way, but had put little store in them. Some said that it was the sun and the moon pulling at the earth, yet only the water would obey. But Ageres had considered himself above such fanciful ideas.

Amazed as he was by the ocean's rise, his attention was quickly distracted by another event of strangeness and beauty. Shining in to the darkness of his cave was a single piercing beam of light from the rising sun. It came through a tiny hole in the cave wall, and shone direct to the rippling water. Yet where it struck the water it scattered in a thousand directions. It spread itself upon the sandy submerged floor of the cave, even as it danced around the walls and roof. It sparkled on the surface of the water and played easily across the lad's skin and wherever these reflections danced and played there was beauty. Every reflection from this single narrow beam was unique; never repeated.

Ageres could see that it was beautiful, but it also moved him in ways he could not understand. The dancing light from the rippling water seemed to wash into him as though he himself were a dark cave. He had no thoughts. There was only room within him for feeling; feeling that rose from deep, hidden places within his core. The feeling grasped at his heart and lungs so that, for a moment, he could not bring his heart to beat or his lungs to breathe, as though he were stone. But a moment later he was released — broken open — by a deep, guttural sob that emerged without warning.

And then he wept; wept like he had never wept before. Not the small weeping of the child; who's weeping is a plea for the care of others. This was, for the first time in his life, the weeping of the man; the weeping that might purge the grief that builds deep in the soul, waiting to be heard.

After many minutes, it passed. And he was empty.

Why did he weep? He could not know, yet. Perhaps exhaustion. Perhaps loneliness, or grief for his childhood. But perhaps, too, for that single beam of light made myriad. Perhaps because he sensed what he could not yet name: this Message, that he had held as the one true light, was but one fleeting reflection of the true light. And if that, then perhaps he wept for the blood and the tears that had been shed by people in centuries past and countries afar; shed for the sake of a dancing reflection of truth that people sought always to capture and freeze, and use against others.

Perhaps. That is the way with weeping. It speaks

of things we have felt deep in our wisdom, but not yet named.

There, in the cave, all he knew was that his weeping was done, and he felt a soft, safe, open emptiness within him that left thoughts unimportant. He slid down into the water that played and sparkled so beautifully in this dark place, and waded through it towards the glaring light of the sand and ocean and sky outside.

Sihdra was waiting, motionless, on the beach. The steam of early morning was rising from her coat and her breath. She stared at the young man as he emerged, and nuzzled at him, seemingly with satisfaction and pleasure, as he came close to embrace her strong, soft neck. He could feel, as though for the first time, the life blood coursing through her veins, the strength resting in her muscles, and the purity shining from her soul.

He walked towards the waters' edge and found rock-pools there, alive with bizarre and colourful life such as he had never seen. He pondered their mysteries, but sought no answers. He threw himself into the bracing waters beyond, and felt his body swayed and rocked and swept along by the hidden powers of this great ocean.

When he emerged, he ran and leapt as Sihdra had done the day before, simply for the pleasure of it. The warmth of the sun and the coolness of the water played on his skin. The hardness of the rock and the softness of the sand caressed his feet. The fragility of the rock-pools and the majesty of the towering cliffs delighted his eyes. He was free.

He picked up a thin piece of driftwood and drew lines in the sand. He ran in wide sweeping circles, round and round and round. And then round and round and round again. And then again. And then again.

And there were the three and the seven. The twelve and the twenty-eight. The Message. On the Edges of the Kingdom. And they were just for him.

"Thank you, Ageres," he said aloud to himself, "for bringing me to this wonderful place. Thank you for showing me your beautiful, magical Rings. I will treasure them always."

And with that he laughed happily and long and loud, and cried some more, and stared at the wide deep ever-moving ocean.

VII

TO HERAAN

"They are very beautiful rings, Sir."

Ageres was startled by the girl's voice. He had been so focussed on drawing his treasured Message in the sand that he had not seen her approach. She was perhaps twelve years old and wore a ragged, flowing robe that brushed the sand. Her face was small and shy, and she looked uncertain about this strange young man. But she went on: "I have seen another draw these rings."

"Where?" Ageres asked in astonishment.

"In my village there is a great table in the square. The communal meals are served there at the changing of the seasons, and many an evening is spent around it, with laughter and stories. These rings are painted on that table."

"Where is your village child?" Ageres's heart was suddenly alive with wonder.

"Two days walk from here; in the Middlelakes. I have come to stay with my aunt and uncle, and to gather sea shells for the market day. I will begin the return journey before the sun is high."

"Child, let me offer you a trade. I will take you with me on that great mare, if you will guide me to your village."

The girl laughed: "I will happily guide you, and need not trade. I think that mare is not for me to ride. Perhaps she could help carry the burdens and gifts that I've collected. But sir, I have people to visit and duties to do on my journey, so it cannot be hurried. You will have to move at my pace."

"So be it," said Ageres. Then, with an embarrassed tone in his voice: "I have another request, and have nothing to offer in return. I am famished, and do not know what can be eaten here. Could you point me to some food?"

The girl giggled at this. "It is strange what treasures can be hidden to the eye." She reached into the nearest pool and pulled out some seaweeds, anemones and small crabs. Swiftly, and with a mumbled prayer, she stabbed the animals and took their life.

"Make a fire, sir, and we will eat well."

Ageres was heartened by the thought of nourishment, and delighted that it could be so easily received. "What is your name, my new young friend?"

"I am named Lodima. But many call me Dima. Use which you will." And she smiled with an openness that brightened the young man's Spirit.

After eating, they began their journey, stopping after a short time at the home of Lodima's aunt and uncle. They were, at first, wary of this stranger and, though offering him food and drink, asked of his origins. He told them of his journey from the City and they were quickly interested, and plied him with questions. They were especially fascinated by his journey through the Emptiness.

Ageres asked of their lives. Dima's uncle explained: "We, too, are of the City, but we have sought silence and solitude in this quieter country between the Ocean and the Middlelakes. You will pass others, today who have done the same."

They would have spoken longer, but Ageres's young guide reminded them that there was a long journey ahead.

By mid-morning Ageres, Sihdra and Lodima were walking along winding paths, overgrown and seldom used. They came, often, to forks and crossroads, but the girl did not hesitate in choosing which path was hers.

From time to time she stopped to deliver sea shells to people who knew her, and who lived in the small huts along the way. She also stopped, occasionally, to make token offerings at special places; a waterfall here, a grand tree there, a small shrine at another place. Ageres admired her quiet competence. She had clarity in her tasks, and an easy knowledge of her way along the labyrinth paths of the tangled forests and wide meadows.

As they walked, Lodima spoke with love of the lands around them, and the plants and animals they saw, and the lives of the people who lived there.

And she spoke of the village that she lived in.

"It is called Heraan. I have not always lived there, but it is all I remember. My parents moved there from the Higher Fells when I was very young. They say they were tired of living amongst people who cared only for themselves. My mother likes to say "In Heraan, we know connection.""

"And do you like the village?" Ageres asked.

"I have friends who I have fun with. We have meadows and shrubbery and wetlands and streams around. They are rich with magic and things to do."

That night they stayed in the home of a large, noisy family. They, also, were related to Lodima and had been expecting her; but not her companion. Again, Ageres was asked of his origins and again, he found welcome once he was known. He learned of their lives, and they learned of his, and all were richer for the learning.

On the second day of their journey, the forests and meadows gave way to a plainer, drier, simpler landscape. As the sun set before them, chased by the silver wisp of a new moon, the three travellers crested the last of a small ridge of hills.

From the crest, they could see, below them, a simple village spread along the side of a lake. The land beyond was gentle and low, with no features to arrest the eye. The colours were of browns and ochres, tinged with wisps of green. The lines of the lake, and the land beyond, and the small huts that made up the village, were low and steady. Only the sky was glorious. And where the red sunset reflected itself in a thousand hues on the lake's surface, there was magic and beauty.

This village did not speak of grandeur, and Ageres was disappointed. Somehow he had imagined the place of the Rings as a remarkable village, in a landscape that would ignite the senses. Yet this was as plain a place as he had seen on his entire journey.

As they followed the path down the hillside, a noise came to them like a gentle stream as it cascades over rocks. But Ageres quickly realised that this was the sound, not of water, but of a hundred voices raised in conversation.

"It's the eve of market day," Lodima said. "Tonight, from sunset, people gather in the village square to talk and argue about all manner of things."

When they reached the edge of the village of Heraan, Sihdra stopped to graze at the meadows. She seemed reluctant to enter the tight busy-ness of the village streets. Ageres understood and walked on with Lodima. But before he had gone ten paces he stopped and looked back at the mare. "Friend, join me in this crowded village, though it may not suit your nature. This may be the moment for which we have travelled so far together. I need your strength beside me."

Sihdra understood his plea through the motion of his eye and hands, and the tone in his voice. She obeyed and they walked on together, Lodima leading the way through this last labyrinth.

As they weaved through the narrow streets of the village, Ageres admired the little houses that lined them. They were made of local mud, and the windows and doors were edged in painted decoration. There were flowers and trees in the decorations, and creatures and birds. There were suns and moons and stars. There was water and fire and earth and wind. There were people, and the things that people made and the things that people treasured. Simple, painted images that spoke of rich lives within.

As they walked, Ageres glimpsed the quiet cacophony of moments that made up those lives. Laughter here, an argument there; children playing and feeding the yard animals and carrying water. Men and women talking, tilling fields and chopping wood. Old folk sitting amongst them, watching the rhythms recur and sometimes change. There was, as there always is, noise and friendship, gossip and ill-will, cruelty and kindness and pervading love. Love that hurt and love that nurtured and love that slowly, gently, painted colour into the line-drawings of living.

Soon the streets opened up into a square filled with people gathered together into small groups, talking and laughing, arguing and questioning, frowning and smiling. In the middle of the square was the 'Great Table', just as Lodima had described. In truth it had been carved from an outcrop of white marble that rose from the earth. Many hands had chiseled the rock into a disc, and ground its surface as smooth as a still lake. And Ageres could see, on that surface, the Rings of his beloved Message. There were the three and the seven, the twelve and the twenty-eight, painted in shining colours.

Lodima led him to a small bench near the Great Table, where six people were engaged in spirited dialogue. She interrupted: "Father, Mother I am back, and I have brought a man who has drawn Casandra's rings in the sand."

Her father stood to shake Ageres's hand with a warm smile. "Welcome to Heraan. You have arrived on a good night. The Market Eve is always busy with talk."

"I think I have never seen so many conversations in one place," laughed Ageres nervously.

"Well there is much to speak of!" Dima's father laughed. "Many of us in this village share just two things: despair about the fading ways of the Kingdom, and hope that there is a way forward. But as you see," he added with a smile and a sweep of his arm, "we do not share the same vision of what that way is!"

Lodima's mother frowned at him: "You diminish us, Hopian. We share much." She turned to Ageres: "Heraan has drawn people who thirst for truth. But they know — or learn when they arrive — that truth is not certainty. No truth is the whole truth, and so we speak and listen in ever deepening exploration. This is why we gather around the Great Table on the Market Eve. This is why you see so much conversation."

There was a pause of agreement, as if the small group of people were breathing her statements in. An older woman spoke into their silence — speaking not just to Ageres but to the small circle of friends:

"It's the great challenge of freedom."

Others, with their silence and their eyes, called her to elaborate. So the woman went on.

"Our Kingdom knows great freedom. Time was when our world kept us safe by showing us one path, and holding us to that path. This left our Spirit safe to live, and sing its song, as we walked the narrow path. But the Spirit yearns for freedom; freedom to choose, and to explore, and to discover new worlds. So that time has passed. The paths that held us have become many and varied, and are now a labyrinth, open to all of us. This is the greatest gift that we have ever received, and the greatest challenge."

"True!" a fourth person chimed in. "The challenge of freedom is simple and deep. Freedom bids us to choose. The many paths are laid before us. And we are free to choose which, if any, we will follow. We must choose, and choose, and choose again as we take our journey through the labyrinth paths of freedom. It is hard, and rich. Never before have we needed such discipline; never before have we been offered such reward."

Everyone nodded, and Dima's father spoke again.

"Yet our Kingdom is crowded with people who are wandering those paths of freedom aimlessly and so are lost. It is crowded with people who are simply following others along the pathways, and so are in the wrong place. It is crowded with people who want all others to follow the same path, and so are bitter. It is crowded with people who are hiding away, and so are choked of pleasure and nourishment.

"But some in our Kingdom are using their freedom to choose. And many of them have come to Heraan to help them choose well. They are standing around you in this Square tonight."

An old man, who had listened silently, turned to Ageres. "Where did you learn of Casandra's rings?"

"*Casandra's* rings?' the Stableboy asked, confused. It was the second time he had heard the name. Young Lodima explained: "Casandra was the woman who painted the rings on the Great Table."

"Ah," Ageres turned back to the old man. "I found them one morning in my heart. I do not know where they came from, but I feel their truth. And I feel the truth of the words within."

At this the man's eyes widened. "You have put

words to the rings? Well this is news indeed!"

"Did this woman, Casandra, not have words to explain the rings?" Ageres asked.

"Casandra was a simple woman," Dima's father replied. "She was more comfortable with children and animals than with adults, and never engaged in our debates. She painted her rings on the Great Table in the days before she died, and spoke only to the children of them."

Lodima added: "She said that she liked the colours and the shapes, and that that's why she painted them."

"Casandra was never one for analysis!" laughed her father. Lodima seemed shaded by his comment, and once again, her mother chided Hopian: "Casandra's rings go to a truth deeper than analysis. They are a poem of shape and colour; the three simplest colours of the world blending to make all the colours of the rainbow.

"The centre of each trinity is pure white, as though it were the one pure light. The beauty of the one pure light is revealed through all the colours of the rainbow and all the colours of the world. And yet all the colours of the rainbow and all the colours of the world only exist because of the one pure light."

Ageres was recalling the light in the cave when

the older man once again addressed him.

"But good sir, you have words for the rings. This is good news indeed, and we must hear the words."

"You must also see the words," Ageres replied, "so I will need paint and card."

"I will paint the words as you speak, Ageres," Lodima said happily, and ran off to one of the houses that bordered the square, returning with a fine brush, a small pot of paint, and rough card.

On her return her father stood, and called for silence in the square, and asked the people to gather around the Great Table.

"Friends, we have a visitor who has brought us words for Casandra's rings. Let us all hear and see."

And so, at last, it was time for Ageres to deliver his Message.

VIII

At the Table

Ageres stepped up on to a stone bench and began to speak, just as he had spoken to the Seafarers.

"Good People: I have a Message."

"From whom?" somebody called. Immediately, Ageres was stalled. The question pierced to the doubt that had lurked within him like a ghostly presence for this whole journey. He was born to shovel shit and straw, to sleep in the presence of bridled beasts. Who was he to be sharing deep truths with this crowd of strangers? The Faereen's curse still sat — hard, sharp and unknown — within him.

"It...I... I think it simply rose within me." he stammered. "I'm sorry. I don't really understand. ... It seems to be given to me to speak it..." He felt like a fool, looked to his feet and prepared to step down.

"Then speak it!"

He looked up, but couldn't see who, from within the crowd, had called that.

"Yes," someone else said. "I want to hear." And those words were immediately followed by a hubbub of agreement. Others, it seemed, also wanted to hear.

So Ageres closed his eyes as though looking

inward, and felt his Spirit move deep into his wisdom, listening for the words of truth that lay there. The rings on the Great Table, and the hushed attention of the Heranians, had given him strength. For the first time on his journey, it felt like the words were emerging through him; not from him. And so he spoke.

"The Message arises from a warning; a warning of distraction. Many in the Kingdom have lost our way. We are distracted by fear and trivia. We are distracted from the simple, beautiful paths that might lead to deeper human living and being. And as each of us lose our way, so all of us lose our way; so the Kingdom loses its way. Lost, we become tired, frantic, powerless, separated.

"We may pursue happiness, or wealth, or love, or power but if we do not, also, develop Spirit we become lost and these pursuits become meaningless.

"So the Message answers the warning with the *Call*, a simple reminder of what is deep in the hearts of all of us: *Develop Spirit*. That Call is at the centre of the Rings, and at the centre of the Message.

"In all that we do, alone and together, we can Develop Spirit. In finding our food, building our shelter; in doing our work, raising our children, playing our games; in our laughter and our crying; our grief and our joy; our arguments and our agreements we can Develop Spirit. We are called to

Develop Spirit.

"Always. And in everything."

He paused, and could see from the many eyes that were trained on him that his words were resonating for many. Then Dima's father spoke: "'Develop Spirit'. These words are good. But not yet clear. Speak of their meaning."

Before Ageres could go on, another voice emerged from the crowd: "The *Ancient Book of Words* gives them meaning!"

It was an elderly man. He had been staring over his spectacles at Ageres with a stern look. His hair and face were grey and stormy, his clothes formal but unkempt, and on his lap was a great and well-worn book. Seeing that he had Ageres's attention he read from the book, in a voice that was low and roughened, like the creaking sound of a door not often opened. "'Spirit', in the tongues of antiquity, is *the breath of life*." Then he looked up at Ageres: "What could be more important? What use happiness, wealth, success, power — even love — if we cannot fully breathe?"

Ageres was amazed to hear this concise explanation for his Message from such ancient and scholarly places. He wondered: was his Message simply saying what is already known? But, encouraged by still expectant faces, he realised that the old man's words led in to the deeper meaning that lay within the

Message. So he continued.

"Yes. And when Spirit breathes we are fully alive — in sadness or happiness, troubled times or calm, in clarity and confusion, at work or at play — when Spirit breathes we are fully alive. Yet when it is choked, all else becomes troubled…"

And so he spoke on, eager to finally share the depth and power behind this word 'Spirit'. He offered the image that, unbeknownst to him, Sophia the seventh advisor had offered King Gabriel. He spoke of the 'drowning' person who cannot breathe their Spirit; who can think only of the next moment; who lashes out; who seeks rescue from beyond rather than within; who gives up. He asked people to reflect on what a Kingdom might look like if it were filled with people thus choked of Spirit. And he asked them to look around at their Kingdom, and understand, then, the importance of developing this breath of life, this Spirit.

"Our Kingdom has slipped toward the silent despair of choked Spirit. Fear, greed, distraction, denial, apathy, hostility, judgement, selfishness — these all seep into the void left when Spirit is choked and cannot breathe. This is how a kingdom decays.

"Yet they are all healed by one means: breathing life into the Spirit of all of us. This is how a kingdom is revived.

"Our Kingdom needs the Spirit of each of us to open and breathe so that it may spread from one person to the next; one community to the next. So that the Kingdom may heal and grow."

The Heranians marveled at the authority with which this young, shy man spoke. They did not know, as Ageres did not know, that the words he offered had been given to him by King Gabriel. For that knowledge had been stolen from his memory by the Faereen's curse. They did not know, as he did not know, that the King's words were, in turn, a simple reflection of the wisdom of Sophia of the Court. And they did not know, as he did not know, that Sophia's wisdom was the emerging inheritance of mothers' mothers.

They did not know all this. But they still listened. They could feel truth in his words. That was the way in Heraan.

So Ageres went on.

"But beware: The Spirit is not something we create. It is not something we teach. It cannot be placed within a person by those around. It rests within, patient and waiting if only we will give it air to breathe. That is why the Call is clear: we are called to '*Develop* Spirit'.

"An important word, *Develop*," said the old Scholar of the stormy face and the ancient book. "The *Ancient Book of Words* makes its meaning clear!"

Ageres noticed that some rolled their eyes. "Ah Scol, too much talk of books might make you boring if you're not careful!" called a young woman from the crowd. There was an eruption of laughter that broke the tension. This man, Scol, went on oblivious.

"Many use it to mean 'change', or 'build', or 'transform'. Not so! The Book takes us back to the ancient wisdom: *Develop* means, simply, 'un-wrap'." And that was all.

Ageres was silent for a moment. Once again, the man and his book offered meanings of simplicity and clarity, as though his Message was little more than a reminder of what is known, but forgotten. But he went on…

"Yes. And so the Message calls us to unwrap the breath of life in each of us and all of us. So that we can see beneath and beyond the next moment, so that we can reach out rather than lashing out; so that we can look for and find our answers within; and so that we can continue to care. Develop Spirit."

And with that, young Lodima, who had already scribed the two words onto card, sprang on to the Great Table, and laid them in the Central Circle of Casandra's Rings.

Many in the crowd moved forward to see these first words — 'Develop Spirit' — laid within the Rings, and the murmuring of many voices began, again, to rise.

But Scol, who had not taken his eyes off the young man, called out. "Well and good lad. Well and good. The Call answers the warning. But the answer begs a question. How?"

This time, though, Ageres was not challenged or shaken by the old man's question. He sensed that this scholar asked because he genuinely wanted to hear. So he closed his eyes, looked inward to the Message, and let its words emerge.

"There are four Tasks; each simple; each essential; each easy to forget or ignore.

"Each, without the others, will fade or fail. All of them, together, can Develop Spirit, in each of us and throughout our Kingdom.

"The first task is to *pay attention.* The first trinity reveals: when I pay attention to my experience and my action and my wisdom I draw out, unwrap, *develop* my Spirit. When I pay attention to your experience and action and wisdom, I help develop your Spirit. And you can develop my Spirit in the same way. Our different truths, abilities and directions emerge and entwine and enrich each other and our Kingdom.

"This simple task is easy to ignore. We can become distracted by our theories, judgements, and assumptions about each other. If we are so distracted, I can choke your Spirit and you can choke mine, and we are both diminished, and our Kingdom is frayed.

So, for yourself, and for others and for the Kingdom: pay attention. On the Rings of your Table, this task is simply *Attend*."

Lodima scribed the word on the next card and laid it at the northern compass point of Casandra's Rings. But Ageres did not notice. He went on to the second task.

"Of course, we cannot do this alone. And if we did, our families and communities and Kingdom could splinter and fray.

"So as we pay attention — as we *Attend* — we must also *Connect*, one to another, so that the parts feed the whole, and the whole feeds the parts, and the Whole Spirit develops. The Trinity of Connection speaks of three disciplines — disciplines that create love, and are, in turn, created by love. Through inquiry, respect and honesty, we create, love. And through that love our lives, our Kingdom and our World are drawn towards wholeness."

Lodima wrote this word, 'Connect' on the next card, and placed it at the eastern point. Few watched her. Their eyes were fixed on Ageres as he went on.

"But these first tasks — of Attention and Connection — will not fully develop Spirit if they focus only on those who are closest to us, or on this time that we are in. We are each a part of something greater. The third and fourth tasks draw us beyond the here, and the now.

"We *Dream* — imagining our life and our Kingdom and our whole world as we wish it to be, and striving to make it so. Each may dream differently, but our myriad dreams are the light of our Kingdom; our striving towards those dreams is the energy that makes the light glow ever brighter and more colourful. We dream of the parts, and we dream of the whole. The trinity of Dreaming reminds us: our dreams for our self, for the I, intertwine with our dreams for others. Our dreams for others intertwine with our dreams for nature. Separate them, and the dreaming fades and splinters. Dream of the *whole*, and each of us is nourished, and Spirit develops.

Again, Lodima wrote—'Dream'—and placed the card to the south. Ageres spoke on, becoming more passionate and assured.

"If we Dream well, we will, alone and together, be inspired towards great visions, and may achieve glorious creations. But what good those creations if they falter and fade for lack of care? So the fourth task fulfills the Call…

"To Develop Spirit we must also *Sustain:* sustain a world in which Spirit can *continue* to breathe, in which we can *all* attend, and connect and dream. The fourth trinity reminds us: we can only sustain our world through justice — through striving for equilibrium between the needs and aspirations of *all* people and *all* beings — ourselves alongside those we know, alongside those we will never meet, alongside those not yet born, alongside the natural world that is the mother of all. Our own Spirit can only breathe well if the Spirit of all beings breathe well. The Spirit of the Kingdom can only develop as far as the Spirit of each of us and all of us develops.

"And so, Justice calls us: live lightly, be compassionate and engage together, for we can only sustain our Kingdom together."

Ageres paused and became aware, once again, of his surrounds. The crowd had held silence as he named the four Tasks, and Lodima was just finishing scribing 'Sustain' onto the card. He watched as she carefully placed it at the western compass point, completing the central words of Casandra's Rings. He felt a growing contentment as he saw the Message that he had carried beginning to emerge with such beauty, and in such a place.

But his contentment was quickly broken.

As soon as the fourth Task had been placed, there was a great surge of voices. People started discussing, debating and discerning the meaning of the words that had been lain on Casandra's Rings. Ageres tried to quieten the crowd, for there was much still to be said. But they would not be hushed. They were too lost in their own conversations with each other to hear his pleas.

He shouted at them: "There is more to hear!" but was rewarded with little more than passing glances.

"Ageres" said a quiet calm voice at his side. It was the child Lodima. "Tell me the words and I will write them, and they will be there for all to see."

"But child," he said, annoyed at her naivety, "they require explanation!"

"Can you not hear? This village is not short of explanations" she laughed. "What it needs is simple truths. Let your words open the simple truths of Casandra's Rings, and let the explanations follow. There will be many!" And her voice rose, again, to a laugh.

Ageres saw that she was right, yet he hesitated. He had enjoyed preaching to these people who seemed so willing to hear. He had started to feel like a prophet of old, but suddenly, again, he was simply a voice within the crowd.

His heart felt heavy as he stepped down from the stone bench. But he did as Lodima suggested, walking around the Great Table with her — he on the ground, she on the table itself — and telling her the words of the Message.

He explained how the three Rings of each trinity

created — in their joining — the seven simple elements of each task. As he did so the four tasks unveiled the twenty-eight elements. And the girl, listening to his words, skipped lightly around the table, scribing and placing the words of his Message in each trinity of rings.

As Ageres and Lodima circled the table, villagers followed them and then peeled off to argue and puzzle over the words that had been added. As they peeled away new villagers would take their place. In this way the arguments and elaborations steadily widened until the square was filled with discussion of attending, connecting, dreaming and sustaining.

Ageres's initial disappointment turned, as they circled the table, to a quiet smile. Nothing was as he imagined it. He had imagined that his quest had been to preach to the people on the very edge of the Kingdom, yet found himself speaking with unknown villagers in the Middlelakes. He had imagined that his quest was to preach to crowds, yet found himself dictating single words to a young girl. He had imagined himself receiving accolades and praise, yet found himself almost invisible in a crowd of dialogue.

But for all that, he began to sense that perhaps his mission had been true, for it had brought him to this very place where, unexpectedly, his Message had been delivered.

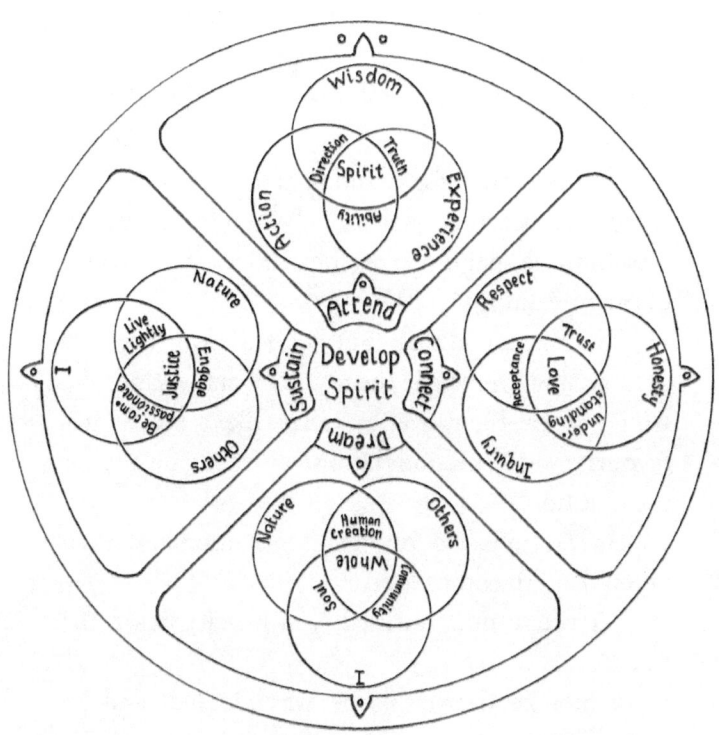

With the words in the Rings complete, Lodima came and stood beside him and stared at the Great Table. "Ageres," she said, "you have brought a poem to old Casandra's rings, and you have brought questions and rich confusion to the village. Casandra would have been pleased. Casandra would have said 'thank you.'"

Ageres stared for a moment at the girl, then responded with a question: "When this woman Casandra was painting the rings, did she give no hint of their meaning?"

"No," said Lodima. "But she had two favourite sayings, and every time she rested from the Rings she would repeat them over and over, like a prayer. My favourite was 'Question the answer when you answer the question.'"

Ageres reflected on that for a moment, then asked "And the other?"

"'If you're not confused, you haven't heard the question.'"

When he heard this he was pleased, and he wandered around the table with a lighter heart. He listened to, and sometimes joined, conversations that were flowing everywhere, and saw a depth in the Rings that he had not known. For he had seen the Rings from only one perspective, yet here they were seen from the many.

Questions danced round the lamplight, and each new answer revealed yet deeper questions until the Rings themselves seemed to be shimmering with life. "How can we know *truth*?" "How can we *inquire* without invading and causing discomfort?" "Who can speak of *soul* without diminishing it to logic?" Some crowded around Scol and his ancient book, searching for the deeper meanings beneath each of the words. And each new meaning, revealed, led to yet more dialogue.

For Ageres, the Message began to change. It began to appear not so much as answers given, but questions revealed; questions that might draw people to reflect on what mattered to them in their lives and their kingdom. Questions that could bring air and light to the Spirit of those who asked, and chose to see. And as the questions shone ever clearer, the Rings seemed to come alive with the music and wisdom of a thousand voices interpreting, arguing, laughing, crying, encouraging and revealing.

Questioning, questioning, questioning.

Just as the first light appeared in the east, the Stableboy left the crowd and walked with Sihdra to the edge of the village, where he lay down in a travellers' shelter and fell to a deep sleep.

He awoke — no dreams at play — when the sun was high. He felt happy; content. He knew it was time to return to his stables, but wanted to farewell Lodima before leaving. So he walked back to the square. He was surprised to find the girl once again on the Great Table, her hand dancing gracefully across the surface.

As he approached and called she looked up briefly and smiled, but quickly refocused on her work. When he got closer he saw that the words had been painted into the Rings in bright golden paint. She was finishing the last of the words as he reached her. It was 'Whole'.

"There was a decision at sunrise," she said happily, leaping lightly down from the Great Table. "They wanted the words painted directly on to Casandra's rings. They asked me to do it." She was alive with the pleasure and the pride of it. And Ageres, too, was pleased.

His work was done, and it was time to leave. He was filled with the quiet, pure melancholy that comes with the completion of a great task. His work was done. His Message delivered.

He took one last look at Casandra's beautiful Rings with their new, golden words, bid young

Lodima a warm farewell, and turned his mind to the return journey.

That is how 'The Rings of Heraan' were born. At least, that's what we call them in the City — those of us who study them. In Heraan, of course, they are, to this day, 'Casandra's Rings'.

IX

Returning

geres was in no hurry now. He returned to Sihdra, brushed her coat, checked her hooves for stones, and led her through a gate to the rich meadow by the village stream where she could graze. For himself, he gathered food, bathed his body and washed his shirt in the clear, flowing water.

The sun was at its highest when he was finally ready to leave. But turning back to take his last look at the humble, beautiful village, he saw Lodima running towards him, her hair and clothes and limbs dancing in the wind.

"Ageres!" she called as she got near. "I wanted to give you a gift!" As she reached him she seemed, for the first time since they had begun their walk together, shy — almost tongue-tied. "You let me lead you through the paths of the Forests. You let me write your words on the Great Table. You made me feel ..." It took her some time to find her words, "like I matter." Her eyes were confused. But she went on. "I would like to give you a memory of me to carry with you as you travel back to the City."

"Lodima!" the Stableboy said with surprise in

his voice. "When I needed food, you fed me. When I felt my journey was ended, you guided me. When I struggled to speak truth, you stood by me. Of course you matter!"

Lodima seemed embarrassed, and turned slightly as she reached for three ribbons of braided threads. One ribbon sat upon her head, holding her flowing hair; one lay around her neck, arcing down as though pointing to her heart, and the third graced her wrist, held there by her young pure hand. Each one was weaved of many threads; gorgeous in colour, bright and fresh.

"Take these threads," young Lodima said; "wear them, Lord, and seek truth where you will."

Ageres laughed. "Not 'Lord' young Dima, just your friend Ageres, the Stableboy!"

Lodima, still embarrassed, seemed, too, a little confused. "My words are jumbled sometimes" she said. As she spoke Ageres felt a slight dizziness and blurring, and for a moment Dima seemed older, taller, even glowing slightly, and her hair flowed like water.

But then he blinked, and looked again, and there was his innocent young friend. 'I must,' he thought, 'find a place to rest early today.'

He looked at the threaded ribbons draped bright across his hand. "Where did you come by these beautiful gifts?"

Lodima shrugged: "I've always had them. Perhaps I was born with them!" she laughed. Then she stretched up to kiss the young man on the cheek, and ran lightly back through the village towards the Great Table.

Ageres watched her go, the ribbons of braided thread still resting in his hand. He looked at them and felt, almost, as though he'd seen them before, but could not remember where. 'I must hold them safe,' he thought, and placed them in the inside pocket of his shirt, close to his heart where they could not be lost, dropped or taken. Then, with a last glance back at Heraan, he swung himself up to Sihdra's back and turned her south towards the Great River.

The path that follows the valley of the Great River is wide and well-trodden. Ageres though, like many younger people, had never had reason to travel it. He assumed it would reveal few surprises, few challenges, few lessons. He knew that it traversed safe, gentle lands, skirting widely around the high wild ranges and the Emptiness beyond. But he was in no hurry now. He had found his truth. He had carried his truth through hardships and emptiness to the very Edges of the Kingdom. He had spoken his truth aloud. He could feel his Spirit alive like never before. He wanted to be by the Great River, where so many others walk. And he wanted to follow it to its source, to the home that was his.

So Sihdra carried him south, and by mid-afternoon they came to the River's slow whispering waters. There they swam, rejoicing in the pleasure of the water's velvet caress. After a quiet rest in the sun's warmth, they turned westward; upstream.

As they walked, Ageres reflected again on the passion with which he had left the City and his stable for the simple cause of speaking truth. He was still bemused by this, for he had no knowledge of the King's quest that had been given to him. That much of the Faereen's curse had held firm.

But he was deeply content. His truth had been spoken and heard, and that truth stood by him and held him strong like a friend might, or a teacher. The long, steady winding path of the Great River suited his contentment well and he sang in hums and whispers as he and the mare travelled its gentle bends. Most others moved quickly along the Path, clearly having business to attend to. But Ageres and Sihdra moved at a more restful pace, as though letting the world pass them by.

He slept long and deep each night, and lost count of the days that they walked.

He had ample times for imaginings and daydreams. Sometimes, when a breeze caught in his hair, he would think back to the dizzying moment when he farewelled young Lodima. There, in his imaginings, a woman remained, with hair flowing like water. His life, as a child, had been lived in harsh and harried surrounds. The soft touch of beauty and deep calm that the fleeting image of the woman brought to his heart was a new and welcome sensation. At first he was uncomfortable with the image, not under-standing. But as the days passed he felt it opening new, richer, deeper places within him so that he began to summons it for his own nourishment, and the world around shone brighter as a result.

Along the Great River there are many travellers' rests, and most evenings Ageres found himself in the company of others. He felt easy with conversa-tion that led where it would. Sometimes it led him to speak of the Rings and of the message. Sometimes he spoke, with quiet and powerful humility, of the Call and of the four tasks and their trinities, and of the beautiful flower of Casandra's Rings that drew the parts to wholeness. Some were seized powerfully by his words. Others stared blankly, and he moved the conversations to other matters.

As time passed on his slow journey home, he began to hear, with surprise, that some had seen the Rings and words before. People told of other travellers they had met on the way; travellers who had spoken of them or even drawn them. It was being said that the Rings were born in a distant village, the words scribed by a twelve year old girl on the whisperings of a passing stranger. Sometimes he confessed that he himself was that passing stranger. Some travellers believed him. Others did not. When they believed him, he felt his heart leap with pleasure, felt himself a little larger than human. When they did not, he felt the shadow of darkness in his heart, but tried to pay it no mind.

One night, while quietly unpacking his day's gatherings of seeds, nuts and berries, he heard, to his surprise and delight, his name being called. "Ageres!" He looked up to see Lodima's mother striding towards him, along with three others from Heraan.

They had a sense of purpose about them, but were clearly pleased to find the young messenger.

"I don't think I told you my name back in Heraan that night," Lodima's mother said as she reached out to greet him. "I am Angelika." And then she introduced each of her three companions: Rasul, Erelah and Anjali. They greeted him in the formal way — hand on heart, and then hand to hand — but their eyes were bright with warmth.

Ageres invited them to join him around the campfire he had lit, and they readied themselves for food and conversation. When they were settled, Ageres asked the question that travellers always ask: "Where are you heading?"

"To the City," Angelika replied. "We have been called there by an Advisor to the Court!"

Ageres's eyes widened to a question, though he did not speak. Rasul, a tall, quiet, angular man, answered. "This Advisor has heard tell of Casandra's Rings. She sent word that Heranians should come to the City to speak of them. She requires us before the new moon."

Ageres was silent for a moment. "And the words?"

Eralah laughed. "The Rings would be silent without the words," she said. "Old Scol made sure none of us forgot that!" And she laughed more, her bright robes and beads rippling with the joy of it. The others met her laughter with wide smiles.

But Ageres did not smile. He stared quietly at the flames. His quietness engaged the others and they waited for him to speak, but he didn't. Finally Anjali broke the silence, carefully. "Are you not pleased that your words found their place?"

"I am. But I am confused. I carried those words, that Message, for many months. I spoke to many people of it. It seemed of little import to most. Then I spoke — it can't have been more than twenty minutes — at the Great Table. Even there, people would not listen to most of the Message. And now it spreads like fire. I don't understand."

Anjali responded. She had gentle eyes and a quiet manner, and held Ageres's gaze as she spoke. "Perhaps not like fire — not so all-consuming. Perhaps more like water. Like mountain rains after a drought, they flow in to dry creek-beds that have lain waiting. "

"But you are right, Ageres" Angelika added. "The message you delivered spreads and grows rapidly. None of us fully understands. It is as if a spell was cast that night — a spell that has unleashed a powerful genie of truth. We in Heraan have pondered over the ingredients of that spell. Of course, your open heart had a power all its own. No message could have been heard without that. But that, it seems, was not enough in other places, in other times, for others' ears. It seems you needed to find Heraan."

"We all needed to find Heraan!" It was Rasul who said this, smiling at the others. "And in Heraan, the many years of dialogue and reflection created the very chalice in which these words could work their magic.

"But also," he went on "Heraan needed the Call. We in Heraan come from many different traditions. We gather and separate around these different traditions. But the Call reminds us of the very essence of every tradition. 'Develop Spirit'. By whatever names — this is at the essence. We can turn to all the countless words and actions of our different traditions and messages and truths and ask this one powerful question: 'Does it develop Spirit, or does it choke it?' No tradition, no belief, no certainty, should hide from the light of that question."

They all nodded, and waited for Rasul's words to settle.

Then Anjali spoke again, turning her focus back to the Stableboy. "Yes. And the Rings; Casandra's Rings. The beautiful Rings that were waiting for your message. Casandra's wisdom was deep. And waiting for us to understand."

Angelika added: "Perhaps that is the way with truth. Perhaps it is most powerful when it finds those in whom it resonates, but who have not yet heard the resonance. Perhaps it is most powerful when we find those who hold our message within, and then speak it. You found Heraan. We were waiting, but did not yet know."

They all fell silent, as if their answer was complete.

But then Eralah spoke, her gaze turned towards Ageres. "And of course, the questions. I could see your disappointment, lad, when the questions arose and you could no longer be heard. But that was the moment that the spell took hold. One thing we have known in Heraan: unquestioned truth shrivels to tyranny. Truth needs questions to keep it strong and free. Truth needs questions if it is to develop Spirit. Truth needs questions.

"The message would have lain thin and brittle without the questions."

They stared quietly at the flames for a few moments, then Angelika turned to Ageres: "I guess that is as much sense as we can make of it so far. Somehow your message of truth spoken on that night, in that place, to those people, released a power that spreads and grows in mysterious ways."

Ageres was pleased by this. "Well: it is good to know that my words are spreading to many places, and growing in their power."

There was an awkward silence, and a troubled dance of the eyes.

Finally Rasul spoke, carefully: "Lad, it is not

your words that are spreading and growing, but the voices of truth. People will speak truth in different languages and with different words."

"So my words, my Message, are meaningless? Empty?"

"Oh no! Your words — your speaking — have power that you have not yet understood!" It was graceful Anjali again. "They were beautiful, true words. But more than this they came through you, not from you. They came from a deeper place that you had glimpsed. It was as if you opened a small, hidden window to the eternal whole. We, listening, glimpsed the light of that place and were drawn to it, as if we could hear God's voice calling."

She fell silent. But after a brief pause, Rasul spoke. "Yes. By speaking you have reminded us and others: we, too, are called to search for and speak for the eternal whole; for what Anjali likes to call 'God'. You have reminded us and others: we, too are called to feel and listen deeply for our tiny glimpse of that eternal whole so that, together, we may know it more fully. The eternal whole has many windows. It speaks in many languages. You have found one window and opened it, using the language you have heard.

"Some may be drawn to your message. Others will seek, and find, different ones. Perhaps those that are true will lead us to different edges of the same place. Perhaps those that are true will lead us towards wholeness."

"Towards God," Anjali said.

"Call it what you will," Rasul responded. "I prefer other names, or perhaps none."

And they both smiled. And nodded.

Ageres felt confused, as though he had heard a riddle that he had not yet understood. But he felt, too, that now the riddle was heard, the understanding might follow.

For now he had no more words, so he rose to place more wood on the flames and prepare his food for the fire. The others were silent for a while, and then began to speak of other matters. They spoke of all manner of things. Life and loves, journeys and stories, nature and beauty. Their speaking was filled with insights and questions and lightness and depth, so that it was late before they finally slept.

When Ageres woke, the sun was already high. The four Heranians had left, for the new moon would appear in two days. But Ageres had not been summonsed and so did not share their haste. He prepared himself and Sihdra as usual, and they walked on.

The last days of the journey were easy and quiet for the mare and the young man. Finally, when the tiniest sliver of moon appeared in the evening sky, Ageres and Sihdra arrived at the foot of the Ring of Mountains that surrounded the High Valley of the City. Here the Great River fell majestically from the Valley's edge, guarded on each side by massive cliffs that soared to towering peaks, flecked with snow.

It was evening and Ageres knew, for all travellers know, that the path across the Ring of Mountains, though well-trodden, was treacherous, steep and tiring and must be climbed in daylight. So he camped there at the base, ate nuts and berries that he had collected through the day and, for the last time on this strange journey, bid his mare Sihdra goodnight

But this night would not be good.

X

The
Second Curse

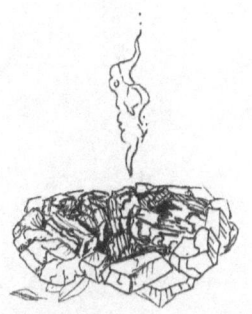

The Faereens that linger just beyond the Ring of Mountains had been, of course, troubled when they encountered travellers carrying a message of Spirit, for Spirit was their nemesis. Troubled, but not panicked. They had seen such messages before, and had watched the messages destroy themselves through the simplest of means: certainty.

They knew that it was powerful, this certainty. Many beautiful truths had been shattered or, better, turned to destruction through the simple certainty that one truth is the whole truth. The Faereens had seen, again and again, rich nourishing dialogue shrivel to sterile debate and contradiction.

They had seen, again and again, the beautiful flesh of truth harden to a brittle shell of rhetoric, and from there to oppression and warfare.

They had seen the very wisdom of faith, which can so liberate the Spirit, twisted to the tyranny of religious law which can so choke it.

And so, at first, they had just waited.

But, to their dismay this truth did not shatter or shrivel or harden or twist, but simply grew. Like a child grows, or a forest. A power had been unleashed that the Faereens could not fathom. It was Spirit. And Spirit was their nemesis.

One Faereen, though, was not just dismayed, but humiliated, for it had seen the message before. This Faereen had strived to choke the message before it was unleashed. This Faereen, in a clearing to the east of the City, had cast a powerful spell of self-doubt upon the sleeping Stableboy. And it had assumed that that spell would be enough. But other spells, it seemed, had intervened; spells of courage and age and mystery and innocence. Spells of wondering and wisdom. And they must have taken hold. For somehow this young man had found the strength to carry the message, and had found a place where the message belonged.

So the Faereen knew, though dared not tell its cousins, that the flow of Spirit that had been unleashed was through its own failing. 'I let it pass,' it thought. As soon as it had heard tell of a message of Rings — the three and the seven; the twelve and the twenty-eight — it knew: 'I let it pass.'

And now, as is the way with Faereens, it had been

drawn back to this lad on whom it had cast its spell. So as Ageres slept by the last embers of his campfire, the leaves and litter of the forest around rustled and shook with the Faereen's troubled presence.

As before, the Faereen listened to the young man's dreams. As before, it saw the Rings in the dreams. But to what avail, now, would a curse of self-doubt be? For by now it was not just the message of Rings that was developing Spirit in the Kingdom, but the very telling of truth that the Rings had spawned.

As before, it chanted to itself, in moaning creaking rhythm: "But it must be stopped and it must be stopped, and the Spirit must be silenced." As before, it searched, in the young man's dreaming, for the cracks of weakness that could be used to take hold of his Spirit.

This time, though, the answer came not in a troubled frown, but in a satisfied smile that played across the young man's face. The Faereen saw: this boy had become man on his journey; his innocence had opened to wisdom. But, as it listened to his dreams, it saw something else. The vital seed that it had planted all those months ago could still bear fruit. For the boy, in his growing, had not become clear on one simple truth: while he had been the messenger, the message did not belong to him. The source of the message — King Gabriel — remained beyond his memory, deeper than his understanding could reach.

So while the Faereen had been unable to stop the Stableboy's power as a messenger, perhaps it could convince the young man that the message was his to control. Perhaps it could convince him that the message was more important than the people who listened. Perhaps it could bring Ageres to don the armour of arrogance, to turn the gift of the message into a weapon of certainty that could be used against the truths of others, and thereby wound and choke, once again, the Spirit of the Kingdom.

And so, again, the Faereen worked a curse upon the sleeping Ageres, whispering words into his dreams:

> *You who've journeyed far and long and seen the ocean's shore;*
>
> *you who've braved the desert's void, and touched upon death's door;*
>
> *you who found these magic Rings, who gave the world this lore;*
>
> *it's you must now ensure they're kept intact!*
>
> *Their Message now can save the world, if the world will only stand and see!*

*Their beauty and their symmetry must stand
untainted, proud and free.*

*And those who'd question God's own truth,
who'd bend and break the four, the three,*

it's they must now behold the simple facts!

*Cast aside what doubts you have, oh strong
and wise, oh chosen one;*

*you alone can bring your peers, your
Kingdom back to truth's great sun.*

*And those who will not follow, drag; and
those who'll speak against you, shun.*

'Til all have seen the light, do not relax!

*There are no other Rings but these; there are
no other sacred words*

*to light the path that must be seen, to play the
tune that must be heard.*

*There is no room for doubt, great man. Be
certain as you travel forward*

and keep the Rings un-tainted and intact!

*Keep them firm and keep them firm.
Keep them firm to shine, to shine.
Keep them firm to shine.*

And the night fell quiet as the Faereen, its spell cast, faded back into the tangled woods around.

But this time it knew there was more to be done. This curse of arrogance it had put on this one man might not, alone, be enough. The curse might ensnare Ageres, as a messenger, in the arrogance of certainty. But what of the listeners? If their wisdom and Spirit was clear, they might discern truth from certainty, and Spirit would breathe yet deeper; the Kingdom awaken yet further. More must be done.

So the Faereen swept through the shadows to alert others of the task ahead. The leaves and branches of the undergrowth cowered and shook in its windy wake. Small creatures tried to shelter themselves from harm.

The message to the other Faereens was simple: they must take to the City; sneak into the cracks and crevices of as many people as they can find. They must hold fast the door to their victims' own wisdom, guard the threshold where stands the quiet discernment of truth. Only then might the listeners spread the disease that the young man's arrogance and certainty would inflict. With Spirits and wisdom closed, they might ignore, and so silence, their own truths. Or they might lash out against Ageres, battling his brittle certainties with their own. Either way: Spirit would falter and fade again, and the Faereens could retain their silent control.

Thus it was that, in the dawning hours of that next day, the City streets were busy with the troubled rustling of a hundred Faereens rushing to do their work.

Having mobilised the others, Ageres's Faereen returned to the young messenger to ensure its work had taken hold. It had learned from the failure of its previous curse that the Spirit of this man could be too easily re-awakened. The Faereen would not, this time, let him out of its sight.

In the new light of dawn, Ageres awoke. And on waking, he found in his heart a new-found determination. These glorious Rings that he had brought to the world filled his mind, and they seemed to enthuse him with a sense of clarity and destiny. The world must hear! The Kingdom must hear! Suddenly he knew that it was only these Rings that could save his Kingdom from the terrible, cancerous decline that had so diminished it through the years of his life.

He had never before felt such certainty. And it made him strong. He quickly ate, gathered his things, bridled his mare, and leapt to her back for their last ride together. He did not know that a Faereen swept along beside him, rejoicing in the brittle arrogance and certainty that its spell had inflicted.

The path to the mountain pass was steep, and worn. Many times Sihdra lost her footing, and she tired quickly, so that, despite his urgings, her pace was slow. By early afternoon he found he had to dismount and lead her to the pass. He was annoyed by her lethargy. 'But what should I expect?' he thought. 'She is simply a beast, and cannot see the importance of what I carry.'

When they finally reached the pass, the view was glorious, and the young man's head was alive with the excitement of what was to come.

At last, as the high sun began its fall towards the horizon, Ageres strode through the streets of the City. He was alone; Sihdra had dropped so far behind that he had lost sight of her. This had not troubled him though. The mare would know the way to her Stable.

Many in the City still remember that day, and students of the Rings of Heraan still honour it. It has come to mark the thin line between truth and tyranny.

Ageres could not have known, of course, why people were crowding the City Square. The 'Rings of Heraan' had, for some weeks, opened dialogue in the City. First a few, and slowly more, had begun speaking of them, drawing them, arguing about them. Ageres could not know that Sophia, the wisest advisor to the King's Court, had called for a Day of Dialogue on the morrow of the new moon, and had invited guests from Heraan to speak of these Rings.

By early afternoon the dialogue was at its peak; the City Square was a symphony of energy and conversation; people everywhere engaged in lively interaction. There was joy and sadness; there was laughter and anger; there was agreement and disagreement. The human Spirit was alive in these conversations, playing and dancing in the clear sun-lit air.

So no-one noticed a determined young man striding towards the crowd.

As he approached the Square, Ageres was, at first, delighted by what he saw and heard. He could see that his Rings had taken hold, and many were speaking of them. Everywhere, the familiar and beautiful symmetry of the Rings had been drawn, with people gathered around them. It seemed clear that he would have many followers. He even glimpsed Angelika across the crowd, though she did not yet see him. She was distracted by others.

As the young man walked on, the Faereen drifted silently in the shadows beside him. It knew that, if the curse of arrogance was to have its true impact, now was the moment. And sure enough, to the Faereen's relief, Ageres's delight was quickly overtaken by anger as he entered the Square. For he saw that many had changed the words within the Rings. And some had even changed the shape of the Rings themselves.

The entire pavement of the Square was a-jumble with bright and faded Rings and words. They were drawn in chalk of many colours — a rainbow of dialogue. But Ageres saw, to his horror, that they were not true to his own vision. Indeed, the very purpose of many of the conversations seemed to be in questioning and revising the Rings, rather than learning from them.

A small cluster of women were pondering over the second trinity. But where the word 'Inquiry' should be, he found 'Deep listening'. "This is not the Rings as they were given!" he complained. And the women looked up, confused, but said nothing.

Another group stood talking around a drawing of the Rings, yet the words 'Choose Hope' had been added to the Call, and 'Vision' had replaced 'Dream' as the third Task. "These words are sacred and are not to be trifled with!" he shouted at them, so that they turned away with fear in their eyes.

Another group had left aside the Trinity of the Dreaming altogether. And still another was, it seemed, redrawing the Rings entirely, using a tangle of lines and arrows, so that Ageres barely recognised them as growing from his Message.

All around were other words — words that did not belong to the Rings yet were connected to them with roughly drawn arrows. Words like power, culture, listening. Words like equanimity, peace, happiness. Strength. Courage. Joy. People seemed intent on invading the sanctity of the Rings by bringing in the words of other teachers, other histories, other peoples.

Everywhere he looked, the Rings were being questioned, and questioned, and questioned again. Ageres was distraught. Had his entire journey been for nothing? Had he risked his very life, only so that people could twist and deform his sacred Message?

He was distracted from these thoughts by raucous laughter, and found a group of loud young people hovering over the Rings. The Rings were intact, but the youth were using them as a game! A stone would be thrown, and where it fell, a challenge was put. "True or False?" they would cry, and the challenged one would tell a story that pertained to the word the stone had found. Was the story true, or false? The young people were wild with hilarious stories, trying to out-do each other with their lunacy.

This was too much for Ageres. He stood in the

circle and kicked at the stone so that it was lost in the legs of the crowd. "How dare you make fun of these sacred Rings! These Rings can change lives. These Rings speak with God's voice! You have no right to turn them into a cheap game!" He was flushed and angry to the point of shaking.

"Ahh man. Leave it be. We're just having fun with words and time. What can it matter to you?"

Ageres lifted his chin and fixed the young men with his stare: "I am the messenger who brought the Rings to the Kingdom. It was *I* who found them, *I* who risked life itself to carry them to the corners of the Kingdom so that they could be heard. *I* am the one who gave the blessed people of Heraan their powerful Message — a Message that will see the Kingdom live again.

"I stand, then, as their guardian, and will not see the Rings desecrated while I have breath."

The youths around raised their chests in defiance. But an older woman who was standing nearby stepped in and spoke quietly, sternly, strongly to Ageres.

"Take your leave, lad. No one is desecrating. These are just rings and words. Who can desecrate rings and words? These words speak of Spirit. But they are not Spirit! They speak of the Whole. But they are not the Whole! Spirit can be desecrated. The Whole can be desecrated. But not mere words. Take your leave."

Ageres became furious. "You don't know what evil you speak. I must tell you so that you will understand. I must tell you all!"

With that, he climbed immediately onto a table and bellowed at the people so that all would listen: "My people, hear me! You are being led astray! These Rings were not given to you for games and questions! These Rings were not given to you so that you might re-draw them as you will, re-name them as you wish! You must stop this foolish talk. I am Ageres. It is from me that these Rings have come. I am Ageres, and I have journeyed far across the Kingdom so that the Rings would find their proper birthplace. I am Ageres, and I stand here now to guard the Rings."

As he spoke, he noticed that Angelika was pushing through the crowd towards him. She seemed to have tears in her eyes. But he paid it no mind. He just went on. "I stand not against you, but for you. For when you see the beauty of the Rings unchanged, when you commit yourself to a life guided by the Rings, *then* you will know true freedom; *then* you will know true joy.

"Stop your foolish chatter! The Rings hold truth for you. You must accept them if you want to find the one true way!"

He would have gone further, for he saw that

he was succeeding at silencing, or in some cases dispersing, the foolish dissenters, but at that point a small man pulled at his cloak.

"What is it man?" he barked impatiently, glaring down at the humble messenger.

"Sir, the King has asked you to join him."

Ageres was amazed and delighted. "*Now,*" he thought "the Rings will find their rightful place in the Kingdom. *Now* the power of them will be understood."

The Faereen, on the other hand, knew suddenly that all could be lost. Gabriel's Court was a place of true power, where no ghostly Faereen could penetrate.

XI

In
Gabriel's Court

The royal castle rose solid and tall at the edge of the City Square, so it was only a short walk to the great, carved wooden gates. As he followed the messenger who had summonsed him, Ageres began to prepare his presentation to the King. He was sure that the King — a wise and noble man by all accounts — would see the beauty, the inviolability of the Rings. More than this, he would have the power to make their words Law through the land. 'Then,' thought Ageres to himself, 'the Rings will be safe from harm.'

He was led up the ancient, foot-worn stone steps and out to the great balcony that overlooked the Square. But as soon as he arrived, he forgot his prepared words, for the King was clearly unhappy; dismayed. And angry.

"Young man! I have watched as you abuse and degrade your fellow citizens; as you desecrate their Spirit. I have watched you deny their search for truth. I have seen you put words and rings above human dignity. I have seen you reduce the beautiful noise of spirited and diverse dialogue to the harsh screech of a single voice, brittle with certainty.

"Just as the Spirit of a thousand voices is beginning to re-invigorate the Kingdom and the City, I see you strive to choke that Spirit. Explain yourself!"

Ageres was shaken by the King's anger, but his certainty held him. He knew he must protect the Rings.

"My King: all you saw me do was defend the Rings that have become the subject of such debate in the City Square. People were insulting them!"

"Not insulting, lad: questioning; exploring."

"It is the same, Lord."

"It is *not* the same. Insult and criticism merely diminish. Questions and explorations nourish, deepen, grow the truths that these Rings put before them."

Ageres, though, was unmoved. The curse in him was strong. He persisted: "There is something you do not know. It was me who found the Rings. They came to me one morning, many months ago now, in a small clearing beyond the Ring of Mountains. It was me who carried them to a village called Heraan, walking through the very shadow of death to take them there. It was me who first revealed the Rings to the good people of that village, and so gave them voice throughout the Kingdom. It is me, Lord, who is called to guard the authority of the Rings."

King Gabriel's eyes softened, though his anger still trembled. "What curse has been cast on you, young Ageres?"

The Stableboy's face creased to startled puzzlement. "You know my name?"

"Ageres," the King replied, "do you not remember standing in this very place, as I revealed the message of my dream to you? Do you not remember that I asked you to take the message to the Edges, so that it would awaken the truth in people's hearts, rather than being feared as a word of law?"

Ageres was, suddenly, deeply confused and disoriented. He stared blankly at the King, his eyes glazed, as if his whole view of the world had been pulled away from him and he could not yet focus on the view that had replaced it.

"Lord, I do not remember."

The King turned his head to the distant mountains. "Then somewhere in your journey, a powerful curse has been draped on you." He said this as though to himself, and kept staring into the distance.

The young man, confused, held his silence until, finally, the King turned back and fixed his eye: "Yet despite this, you have carried the message and you have set it free. Your courage is clearly great, and you have done the Kingdom the greatest service: you have spoken truth, so that others may hear, and question, and speak theirs. So do not, young man, destroy your work by choking the truth of others!"

"But Lord," Ageres replied, struggling to find focus again. "If these Rings are the Message of the King then, surely, they are sacred beyond all other truths. Then, surely, they are the greatest of truths in our Kingdom. If you have dreamed them, surely they must be guarded against the mere ponderings of your subjects."

"Ageres," the King replied, stepping close to place a firm hand on his young messenger's shoulder. "I have dreamed many times, since I dreamed these Rings. I have heard truth in many forms. And I have sent out other messengers. You may have been the first to have spoken your message to those who would hear. But there will be others."

"My Kingdom has begun to find its voice again. But the voice of a kingdom cannot be the voice of one. It must be the voice of many, or the Spirit will be choked. You say you are a guardian of the Rings. Words and rings do not need guardians. They need agents. Words and rings are there to be carried and spoken and heard and questioned; not to be guarded. Be an agent for the Rings, Ageres; not a guardian. If you would guard, guard truth. Guard justice."

Ageres stepped back. "But Lord! 'Truth' and 'Justice' are held by the Rings! That's why I must be their Guardian!"

Gabriel's frustration rose again: "Listen, Ageres! Truth and Justice are held in many messages, not just yours. They are more than mere words.

"You will guard *truth* when you guard the freedom of all to speak freely and thoughtfully of their own truth. If you seek to guard mere words and rings, mere theory and rhetoric, then you stand *against* truth; you choke the questions and answers of others.

"You will guard *justice* when you strive to sustain and balance the needs that keep the Kingdom whole. Develop Spirit, lad, for it is only spirited people who will serve each other, and it is only spirited people who will refuse to be crushed. It is only spirited people who will question before criticising; who will explore before insulting."

The King's anger was subsiding, though his passion was still clear.

"Hold the Rings dear, Ageres, as I do. But hold them lightly, and rejoice in the questions that grow from them."

Ageres felt wisdom in the Kings words. But the Faereen's second curse still held, so that there remained, within him, a grinding certainty. The Rings were too important, too self-evident, too complete in their symmetry to be compromised by others. This certainty rose to the surface and, once again, he became agitated and angry.

"Lord, you must see, again, the power of these Rings. I fear you have been distracted and waylaid. There can be no other truths but these — they hold all other truth within them. They hold the three pure colours of nature. They hold the four points of the compass. They hold the seven days of the week. They hold the twelve months of the year, the twenty-eight days of the moon's re-birth. Lord, the Rings are complete. I will not leave here until you have seen the error of your uncertainty!"

The King, though, remained calm. "I know your passion, lad. I felt it too when first I saw the Rings in my dream. Yet I, in turn, was drawn back from certainty to truth, by the person who had given me the rings, but in different form. She is now my senior Adviser. Her name is Sophia, and it was her gift of words, and of three woven ribbons, that sparked the fire of my dreams."

Ageres was astounded. He reached deep into the inner pocket of his vest; reached for the ribbons that he had forgotten were there. "Ribbons such as these, sir?"

"Ah, so you still have them. I thought you must have lost them if our last meeting had been lost to you."

Ageres was puzzled by the King's words yet again. "Sir, these were given to me by a girl who guided me through labyrinth pathways from the ocean to the village of Heraan."

At this, the King laughed in surprise and called for his senior Adviser. A minute later a beautiful woman walked into Gabriel's Court, her hair flowing like water. Again, Ageres stared blankly. Again, the world seemed to change shape in front of his eyes. For here before him stood the woman who's image had shimmered and glistened behind young Lodima when she had farewelled him.

The King spoke first, to Sophia. "It seems Ageres has lost your ribbons, and found them again." Speechless, Ageres handed the ribbons to Sophia, who cradled them in her hands, then stared at his eyes and spoke.

"I see you have travelled far. These are ribbons such as mine; handed down by the mothers' mothers. Yet they are different, for these have been woven with innocence, while mine were aged with knowledge. Your journey was a rich one indeed. Welcome back, Ageres."

She slipped one ribbon over her hand, hung the second around her neck, and wrapped the third around the hair of her head. Then she leant and kissed him lightly on the cheek saying, again, "Welcome back, Ageres. Welcome back from your labyrinth pathways of knowledge and innocence." There was lightness in her words, but also warmth. "Dine with me, and we will speak of your journey"

And with the feel of her kiss on his cheek, clarity and memory returned to Ageres. As though seeing a glorious view through a clearing mist, he saw, for the first time, his journey in its completeness. He recalled, clearly, the first meeting with the King; recalled the power of the Message as he first heard it and his excitement as he passed beyond the Ring of Mountains. Yet he recalled, also, those for whom the Rings held little nourishment. The Gnomic Woman in the forest; The Old Man of the Emptiness; the Edgelings and the Seafarers. He recalled the humility he had felt when he had delivered his message to the people of Heraan. He even felt, with a shock, the shadowy tremor of the Faereen that had taken hold of him and had tried, and tried again, to choke truth however it could.

And he stared back at Sophia, and felt, for the first time in his life, truly complete.

EPILOGUE

Sophia and Ageres dined together that night, and spoke long. Over time, friendship and then love grew and deepened.

This is not the place to speak of their courting, but it nourished their Spirits and made them whole. She loved to hear of his actions and experiences. He loved to hear of her wisdom.

Eventually they married, and lived together in a cottage by the stables. Joined, they led their lives in the service of the *Trinity of Attending*. A painted image of it hung above their hearth.

Ageres cared for the horses and sometimes carried messages to the corners of the Kingdom. He loved to speak and question with others on matters of Spirit, and often joined in dialogue around the Rings of Heraan. Many sought his counsel over the years, and he offered it freely.

Sophia remained as adviser to the King Gabriel, and to the Queen who followed, twelve years on. Gabriel lived out his reign in peace, content in the knowledge that his Kingdom had, once more, begun to see, to hear, to speak and to breathe open and strong, as a Kingdom should.

The Spirit of our Kingdom has flourished since. It is alive with the passion of attending and connecting, dreaming and sustaining. These gifts abound throughout the Kingdom, and within each person. They are freely there for the taking and giving, at least for those who choose to see.

THE END

AFTERWORD

To you who may read this…..

Wistoria's account of Ageres's journey was written some generations back. The Spirit unleashed at that time has lived on. The Rings themselves, having done their work, have faded from view for many, though others love them still. We in Heraan celebrate them to this day.

Alas, the oceans are rising around us now, even as the sky offers too little rain. We do not yet understand the reasons, but the results are becoming plain. Our lowlands are disappearing beneath the waves, our middle lands becoming too parched and dry for life. Many are leaving for unknown places. Others are mired in conflict. We hope to survive, but cannot be sure. So I have decided to cast a copy of our *Heranian Collection* — including Wistoria's account — to the oceans. Even if the worst should happen, as some are predicting, we can take comfort that the Rings, and the story of their birth, may awaken Spirit in other lands and times, as they have in ours.

You who may read this story, live your life well. Speak your truth to those in whom it resonates. Listen for truth that resonates within you. In all that you do, Develop Spirit.

And think of us; rejoice with us here in the Kingdom. Our Spirit breathes long and deep. Ageres, Sophia, the King, the Old Man, and the ever-arguing villagers of Heraan are still here. The Gnomic woman and Lemma, the Seafarers and their dragons, Mustes and Lodima and, most of all, Sihdra have lived, happily, ever after.

Perhaps they also live on within you, if you will only choose to see.

With love,
Transitus of Heraan.

Translator's Note:

Book II — The Abridged Collection.

The manuscript I found on that wild winter's beach held two parts. The first was what you have just read: Wistoria's account of *The Stableboy's Journey*.

The second was longer. Entitled *The Abridged Collection*, it appears to have been created — over many lifetimes — in response to Casandra's Rings. I'm in the process of translating this *Collection*, though it's a large body of work.

I have included just one entry here; an entry I particularly like, and that suggests that the Rings came to hold an important place in the community life of Heraan.

THE HERANIAN RITUAL
OF ORDER AND CHAOS

This "prayer" and ritual involves the whole village on the anniversary of Ageres's arrival in Heraan.

The villagers stand in a great circle that fills the village square. Four 'element holders' each stand at one Trinity of the Great Table: earth (holding a bowl of fine dust) at the trinity of Attention; water (holding a bowl of water) at the trinity of Connection; air (holding bellows) at the Trinity of Dreaming; and fire (holding a flaming torch) at the trinity of Sustaining.

A Child, aged 12, stands in the middle of the Great Table — in the Circle of the Call.

The prayer is recited very formally, the questions and responses spoken carefully and clearly.

(Child)	<u>What must we do?</u>
(ALL)	DEVELOP SPIRIT
(Child)	<u>How shall we do this?</u>
(Holder of earth)	Through attending
(Holder of water)	Through connecting
(Holder of the air)	Through dreaming
(Holder of fire)	Through sustaining

(ALL)	WHAT SHALL WE ATTEND TO?
(Holder of the earth)	Experience, Action and Wisdom.
(ALL)	WHAT SHALL BE OUR REWARD?
(Holder of the earth)	Clarity in our Ability, Truth and Direction. Clarity of Spirit.
(ALL)	HOW SHALL WE CONNECT?
(Holder of the water)	Through three Disciplines: Inquiry; Respect Honesty.
(ALL)	WHAT SHALL BE OUR REWARDS?
(Holder of the water)	Acceptance, Understanding, Trust, and thereby Love.
(ALL)	WHAT SHALL WE DREAM OF?
(Holder of the air)	Of the I, of others, and of Nature.
(ALL)	WHAT SHALL BE OUR REWARD?
(Holder of the air)	The pleasure of community, of human creation, and of soul. Glimpses of the Whole.
(ALL)	WHAT SHALL WE STRIVE TO SUSTAIN?

(Holder of the fire)	All that is needed by the I, by Others and by Nature, now and forever.
(ALL)	HOW SHALL WE SUSTAIN THESE NEEDS?
(Holder of the fire)	Live lightly, be compassionate and engage together, balancing the needs of all.
(ALL)	WHAT SHALL BE OUR REWARD?
(Holder of the fire)	A world of Justice; for us and for generations to come.
(Child)	And what, then, shall be our ultimate reward?
(ALL)	LIVES OF SPIRIT A COMMUNITY OF SPIRIT A KINGDOM OF SPIRIT GOD MADE WHOLE.
(Child)	Is this the one true way?
(All: shouting)	Nooooo!!!!!!!!!!!!!!!

On the shout of "No" chaos erupts. The holders of the elements and all who choose to join them try to chase and 'defeat' one of the other elements. The water can douse fire, the fire can burn the bellows, the bellows can scatter dust, and the dust can misplace the water.

And everyone can break the rules — the elements can turn on others in entirely unexpected ways. In this way we remind ourselves that, although the Rings look neat and certain, life is not so.

In this way, also, we have really good fun.

ACKNOWLEDGEMENTS

Thanks to...

Peta Wellstead, for your editing — patient, clear and always valuable. And for being the 'Gnomic woman' in my own stumbling journey towards Heraan.

Joy Benz, for your passion and creativity in illustrating this tale.

Neil McLeod, for your forensic proof-reading and your perfect drawing of 'The Rings'.

Maarten van der Wall, Jen de Vries, Antonia Hendrick, and Kathy Al-Kaisi for taking the time to read, and offering encouragement.

David Nourish — Seafarer of the soul — for being my guide, friend, mentor and co-traveller on the tangled pathways of truth-telling.

Anthony Kelly, for urging me to find the Message in the first place.

The hundreds of people whose enthusiasm for 'developing spirit' made this book seem worthwhile.

And finally and forever, Liza Anne Pickering, for your love and support. And for saying I do.

ABOUT THE AUTHOR

Tim Muirhead has worked in, and written about, community development and cross-cultural relations for over 30 years. In that work he has focussed, particularly, on how we develop the human spirit in each of us and all of us.

He is the author of *Weaving Tapestries: A Handbook for Building Communities.*

He lives in Perth, Western Australia.

If you are interested in more reflections or dialogue about the 'Rings of Heraan', please look for 'Finding Heraan' on Facebook.